CHANGING TIDES

❧ *A* GATES *Family Mystery* ❧

By Catherine Hapka

Based on characters created for the theatrical

motion picture "National Treasure"

Screenplay by Jim Kouf and Cormac Wibberley & Marianne Wibberley

Story by Jim Kouf and Oren Aviv & Charles Segars

DISNEP PRESS

New York

Thank you to those who started this hunt:
Oren Aviv, Charles Segars, Jim Kouf, and Jason Reed

And those who carried it on:
Christine Cadena, Rich Thomas, Kari Sutherland,
Eunie Jung, and Elizabeth Rudnick

CHANGING TIDES

❧ *A* GATES *Family Mystery* ❧

Copyright © 2007 Disney Enterprises, Inc.

All rights reserved. Published by Disney Press, an imprint of Disney Book Group.
No part of this book may be reproduced or transmitted in any form or by
any means, electronic or mechanical, including photocopying, recording, or by any
information storage and retrieval system, without written permission from the
publisher. For information address Disney Press, 114 Fifth Avenue,
New York, New York 10011-5690.

Printed in the United States of America

First Edition
1 3 5 7 9 10 8 6 4 2

Library of Congress Catalog Card Number on file
ISBN-13: 978-1-4231-0814-6
ISBN-10: 1-4231-0814-0

This book is set in 13-point Centaur MT

Visit disneybooks.com

London, 1612

"**W**here are you off to, then, son?"

Samuel Thomas Gates paused at the threshold of his family's flat. His father was smiling at him from the doorway of the back room. Dressed in breeches and a linen shirt, Benjamin Gates's thin shoulders were stooped, his pale brown hair was messy, and flecks of that morning's meal dotted his untrimmed beard. He held a metal escapement in one hand and a clock casing in the other. While it was a holiday and the shops were closed, Benjamin was a clockmaker by avocation as well as by trade. Even in his off-hours, he liked nothing better than tinkering with the intricate innards of one of his timepieces.

Since turning eighteen earlier that year, Sam sometimes had the unsettling feeling of peering into a looking glass when facing his father. They were now of equal height, and except for a few extra wrinkles around the father's eyes and a bit less hair at the temples, looked much alike.

"I'm going to the theater, Father," Sam said, adding quickly, "I have the sixpence to pay my way—a gentleman gave me it as a tip at the shop last week."

Benjamin laughed. "No need to worry about that, my lad. If things go as I think they shall, you'll soon be able to attend the theater every day if you so wish. And be seated in a fine box, no less." He gave a broad wink. "What is the play today?"

Sam was glad to see his father in such good spirits. Benjamin had been hinting lately of a mysterious financial windfall, though the rest of the family knew better than to ask too many questions. Sam only hoped he was aiming to sell one of the finely crafted clocks he'd been working on to a wealthy gentleman, rather than hoping—yet again—to procure a fortune through some harebrained scheme. Benjamin Gates was one of the cleverest men Sam knew, as well as one of the kindest, but he could be troublingly naive in matters of money. That was one reason why the furniture in the flat was threadbare and the family's clothes patched over and over until they fell apart entirely.

"It is the latest by Mr. Shakespeare," Sam answered. "*The Tempest*, I believe he calls it. I know little of the plot, but I did enjoy his *Macbeth* when I saw it performed last year."

Benjamin smiled broader and dropped a hand on Sam's shoulder. "I suppose it matters not what the play is, eh, so long as the company is agreeable?" He winked again. "Will young Miss Sarah Moore be attending, do you suppose?"

Sam felt his cheeks blush crimson. It shouldn't have come as a surprise that his father was aware of Sam's affections. Benjamin had a head for puzzles and mysteries and secrets of all kinds. Not only could he fix any clock or other mechanical device there was, but he enjoyed working codes and could guess the ending of nearly any book or play before it was half over. Which meant keeping secrets around him was a rather difficult task.

"I had best be off," Sam said hurriedly, not bothering to answer his father's question. "I'll want to arrive early to find myself a proper spot in the yard near the stage."

"Get along with you, then," Benjamin said, cuffing him good-naturedly on the shoulder. "Have a fine time at your theater."

"Thanks, Father." Sam hurried out the door and onto the street outside, humming under his breath all the while. He barely noticed the familiar sights, sounds, and smells of the city, or paid any mind as he dodged two dogs fighting noisily in the street. His father had seemed pleased by the idea that Sam might fancy Sarah Moore. That was a relief; Sam had feared he might disapprove of such a match. After all, her family was much better off than their own.

Then again, why should Father disapprove of such a thing as that? Sam thought as he waited for a four-in-hand to trot past before continuing across the street. *It is what he did himself— married a woman well above his station. And Mother says she has never regretted a moment of it.*

He smiled fondly as he thought of his mother, Alice, toiling on in the modest flat without complaint, stretching every penny as far as it would go. While Benjamin had always managed to eke out a modest living with his clocks, he could be too much the perfectionist and rather slow, which made money tight. Sam and his elder brother, William, did what they could to help. Sam was apprenticed at a bookbinder's shop, and William brought in a steady, though modest, income as a laborer. So things weren't *too* terrible. Perhaps it was time to broach the subject of an official courtship. After all, Sam was eighteen now—more than man enough to strike out on his own.

Of course, marriage to a humble shopboy may not please Sarah's father, even if she is willing to take me as I am, he thought with a twinge of anxiety. *If only there was some way to pay for a real education, I know that would raise my status. . . .*

His gaze flickered over to a nearby building and landed on a familiar broadsheet hanging on the side. The Virginia Company had been advertising all over London for would-be colonists, promising volunteers a share in the riches of the New World across the ocean. Sam had heard the tales William had brought back from the docks—tales of gold gleaming out from every bit of rock, jewels tumbling in upon the shore with the strong ocean waves, even precious minerals dripping from the trees.

For a moment, he drifted to a stop in front of the broadsheet, contemplating all he could do with such wealth. He would be able to attend Oxford. There he could study history, Greek, astronomy, and more. For as long as he could remember, Sam had burned to know more of the larger world outside the few humble London blocks that made up his own entire existence. His mother, who had received more education than many ladies, had taught him to read and write as a small boy, and he took whatever spare time he had to read the books that passed through the shop. Books by learned and worldly men of the day, such as Sir Walter Raleigh, John Donne, Captain John Smith, the late Christopher Marlowe, and even the brand-new English translation of the great novel of the Spaniard, Cervantes, among others. Sometimes he felt as if he would never have time enough to read all he would like.

But all that would be different if he had even a small share of those New World riches. What's more, as a wealthy, educated man, he would be able to court Sarah in the way she deserved. He would be able to afford a horse and carriage, a fine house for his whole family, all the clock parts his father could want, and a staff of servants, including a maidservant whose only task would be to wait on his weary mother's every need.

After a moment, he sighed and moved on, chiding himself for such foolish daydreams. What did one such as he know of such fortune-hunting? He was no stout and sturdy adventurer. He was merely a shopboy, pale of skin and rather weak of limb—as burly William delighted in proving in his frequent challenges to impromptu wrestling matches.

And then there was Sarah herself. Though Sam had

heard that girls and women were now among the colonists in the New World, he couldn't imagine Sarah among them, with her fine clothes and love of the theater. And she had many admirers—if he went off to the New World without her, it seemed quite unlikely that she would still be waiting for him when he returned.

No, it was madness to think of such things—that sort of dreaming was what always earned his father snickers from the neighbors. He should try to be more like William, who seemed perfectly content in his simple life of hard labor, deep sleep, and a nip of strong ale in between.

Soon Sam reached the Globe Theater, its three-story octagonal walls and the thatched roof covering the galleries towering grandly over its neighbors in the rather lowbrow Southwark district along the Thames. Paying his admission, Sam made his way to the crowded pit in front of the raised stage, where he jostled for position among the sailors, laborers, and miscellaneous groundlings who had gathered for an afternoon at the theater. His shoes crunched on the hazelnut shells underfoot as he found a spot only a few bodies back from the edge of the stage. Several members of the actors' company were busy arranging props upon the stage for the coming performance.

"Look!" a man standing nearby shouted, pointing at the stage. "Isn't that Mr. Shakespeare himself?"

"It is!" another playgoer cried out. "Oi! Oi! Playwright!"

A number of others nearby began calling out and tossing hazelnuts at the slight, bearded figure on the stage. The playwright scurried out of range and cursed at them, causing much laughter among the groundlings. Sam watched as Mr. Shakespeare bustled off with the other members of the company. But he was less interested in the celebrated writer and actor than in someone else.

Turning away from the stage, he raised his eyes to the lowest level of roofed galleries above, searching for a certain familiar face. He smiled when he spotted Sarah. She was sitting with her sisters, looking like a china doll with her pale skin and hair, her heart-shaped face framed by her high collar and lace bodice. After a moment she must have felt his gaze. Meeting his eyes, she wriggled her fingers in a wave. He waved back vigorously.

"Watch it, mate," the man beside him grumbled, as Sam accidentally bumped him.

But Sam hardly noticed. Just seeing Sarah had lifted his

spirits. The Gates family might not be wealthy, but it was hardworking and respectable. Surely Sarah's father would come to appreciate that.

In any case, Sam was determined that it was indeed time to make his intentions known, come what may. No turning back.

Sam was still in a good mood as he walked home after the play. The performance had been a fine one, filled with humor and drama. Sam found it a wonder that it had been written by a man so much like an older version of himself. Hadn't Mr. Shakespeare, too, come from humble beginnings? Didn't he, too, lack much in the way of formal education?

And yet look what a life he has made for himself here in London, Sam thought as he walked. *All from a deep love of words and the theater. If only Father's love of timepieces could make him as well off as that, or my interest in books and knowledge . . .*

His thoughts were interrupted by a great shouting from his flat just ahead. It was William's voice, and he sounded as angry as Sam had ever heard him, though he couldn't make out his words. Sam put on speed, wondering if his brother had surprised a thief in their home—for what else could rouse William's even temper?—and burst into the flat.

"What is it?" he cried. He glanced around for the thief or other interloper, but saw only his family gathered in the main room. William's broad, handsome face was bright red beneath its shock of black hair. Benjamin stood before him in silence, looking small, pale, and slight before his brawny eldest son. Alice Gates was nearby, her face streaked with tears.

"Samuel," Alice cried when he entered. "Oh, Samuel!"

"What is the matter?" Sam asked, his heart racing. "William, why are you shouting?"

William strode toward him, his expression so dark and angry that Sam took a half step backward. "Ask him!" William roared, jabbing a finger in their father's direction. "He's the one who has ruined the Gates name!"

Benjamin raised both hands before him. "Please, son," he began weakly. "I thought this would help all of us. How was I to know that man was a charlatan? He seemed most sincere."

"Father?" Sam's body went cold as he recalled Benjamin's earlier comments about money. "What have you done?"

Between Benjamin's stuttering and William's shouting, he soon had the answer. Unbeknownst to any of them, Benjamin had invested in an expedition to the New World. He had used not only all of the very modest Gates fortune, but had also borrowed from several wealthy customers to raise the money required by the man he'd met at the local pub. This man had led him to believe that he would be sponsoring a group of adventurers who would bring back riches beyond imagining . . .

". . . like the riches found by the Spanish not long ago," Benjamin finished, his eyes distant.

William shook his head, still scowling. "Instead, the charlatan disappeared, never to be heard from again," he spat out. "He took our money and ran. Riches beyond imagining, all right. Enough for that scoundrel!"

"But how do you know he is a scoundrel?" Sam's mind jumped back to that broadsheet with its promise of untold wealth. "Could the expedition be real?"

William shot him a look of disgust. "You sound like Father."

Sam shrank back. He knew his father was a dreamer, impractical verging on foolish. But was he, himself, really the same, with his dreams of education and a bright future? Is that how his brother viewed him? Is that how *others* viewed him?

"It is not real, Sam," Benjamin said quietly. "William has learned the truth from an acquaintance just this day."

"I wager this puts an end to your wasting money on plays and books and such, little brother," William snapped, his voice dripping with disapproval.

"Yes," he said slowly. This had not been one of his father's usual small schemes, risking just a few pounds here or there. This was different. "I guess it's the end of all such pleasures."

Benjamin turned to Sam, despair in his eyes. "I did it for all of us, Sam. Can you see that?" he said. "I was going to send you to university. . . ."

Sam wanted to do as he'd done time and again—to smile and say it was all right, that they would muddle through somehow. But how could he? His father had ruined them all—and their family name. It was one thing to be a pauper; quite another to be known as a debtor and a fool.

"Sam?" Benjamin pleaded. "My boy?"

His heart breaking, Sam shook his head and turned

away to escape his father's eyes. There was nothing to say.

Sarah will never look at me again once she hears of this, he thought. *The name Gates will be spoken with nothing but mockery, and I shan't be able to show my face anywhere in London. I'll be lucky if Mr. Wesley will still have me at the shop once the wags start with their gossip.*

He glanced at his irate brother and his weeping mother, who hadn't said a word since his arrival. No, this mistake would not soon be fixed.

Risking a quick glance at his father, he saw that Benjamin had his head in his hands. Sam quickly looked away again. His father was so good at guessing the outcome of the plots of silly novels and plays. So how could he be so terrible at it in real life?

One

Sam closed his eyes and braced himself as a stiff wind blew over the deck of the *Susan Constant*, stinging his face with salt spray. The sun had set over the watery horizon some time ago, but the moon was out, and the group of half a dozen men who had gathered at one end of the deck, as much out of the sailors' way as was possible on the crowded ship, showed no signs that they were yet thinking of sleep.

"Tell us another one, Jasper!" William shouted, lifting his mug of grog overhead. "I wish to hear more about this Treasure of the Ancients. Explain to us again why it was spirited off to the wilds of .the New World rather than stored or spent in the courts of London or Paris or Madrid? Too great for one man—was that what you said?" He grinned and pounded his chest. "Perhaps only because they hadn't met *this* man! I'd make good use of any treasure, I would!"

"Mock me not," Jasper Riggs replied with a sly grin, as

the other listeners roared with laughter. "Else I shall feel no need to think of you when I'm dining with King James as he begs me for a loan—or perhaps when I am sitting upon my golden throne as discoverer of the fabled City of Gold."

From his spot on the deck, Sam leaned forward, eager to hear more. Jasper, a bone-thin, hook-nosed, dark-haired man of about thirty, made him a little nervous—there was something a bit too cunning in his eyes—but Sam loved hearing his tales of legendary treasures. He got the same feeling from such stories as he once had when lost in an exciting play or book of adventures—two things he did not expect to see again soon.

An older man with a patchy gray beard and large, protruding ears was watching from his seat upon a barrel nearby, leaning forward to listen in between long drinks of grog. "You keep searching for such mythical treasures if you like, Riggs," he said, his words slurring slightly. "That leaves the true treasure for those of us who know where to look."

Jasper shot the other man a condescending look. "Ah, yes," he said, leaning back against the stiff ropes leading up to one of the masts. "The *true* treasure. Are you planning to tell us more, Turner, or merely continue gloating over your so-called secret knowledge of a so-called treasure?"

Sam winced on behalf of the older man. Elias Turner, like Jasper, seemed certain that he would make his fortune in the New World by discovering treasure, and as such, the two had argued incessantly since boarding about which of them would do so first and most gloriously. However, Sam found himself much more sympathetic with Elias's quest than with Jasper's—perhaps because he found Elias himself much more agreeable.

He'd had plenty of time to get to know both of them, along with everyone else onboard the ship. The *Susan Constant* was better than two-thirds of the way through the six-week journey to the New World, specifically Jamestown Settlement in the Virginia colony. Sam and William Gates were among the group of settlers making the trip. It had been Sam's idea to sign on with the Virginia Company— after all, anything would be better than remaining in London once word of Benjamin's folly had spread—and it had taken little to convince William to come as well. The company would pay their way in exchange for a few years' labor, and in return, the Gates brothers earned the chance to start fresh in a place where their name meant nothing, good or bad. And if they found enough success in the colony, they could send for their parents and rescue them from their dreary life of absolute poverty in London.

"The New World ruined the family," Sam had told William after bringing him to look at one of the broadsheets on their street. "Why not see whether it might also be our salvation?"

Sam's old dreams—of formal education, of Sarah, of respectability—had disappeared nearly as quickly and completely as the family's fortunes, only to be replaced by this new one. He'd always dreamed of bigger and better things, far-fetched, impossible things like Oxford. Why not this instead? True, he was slight of build and inexperienced with much outside his own sphere, other than through the books he'd read. But he was also smart and determined and willing to learn. And even a fortnight in the New World would surely teach him more about life than all the books he could read in a year.

Which is how they found themselves aboard the very same ship that had carried the first settlers to Jamestown some five years earlier. Sam had taken that coincidence as an omen, a sign of luck in their new venture.

Life on the ship was uncomfortable and dull, and the passengers had only one another for entertainment. Sam had soon discovered that many of his shipmates were somber settlers full of practical and modest goals for their new home. So he and William, along with a handful of other young passengers, had gravitated to Elias and Jasper, who often stayed up late drinking and trading tall tales of lost gold and treasures beyond imagining.

"Even if this Treasure of the Ancients is real, what makes you think it's anywhere near Jamestown Settlement?" one of the other listeners, a wiry young man known as Red for his shock of auburn hair, asked Jasper now.

"Right," William put in. "The New World is said to go on forever, with thick woods and unfriendly natives, and wild creatures the likes of which you've never seen."

Jasper tipped the last of his grog into his mouth and then smiled, licking his thin lips. "If the treasure were easy to find, it would already be found," he said. "I expect it might take some time for me to search it out. But I'll have plenty once we reach the shores."

Sam's gaze wandered out toward the endless rolling waves, which were lit only by a pale, cloud-shrouded moon.

All the vivid descriptions of the New World he had heard since boarding had set off his imagination. Every creak and shudder of the ship's hull sounded to him like wild animals creeping through the underbrush, and the shadowy figures of the crew moving about the rigging could pass for savages preparing to attack. Although Sam knew very well that such images weren't real, they would be real enough soon—in a matter of weeks now, he, Samuel Thomas Gates, an ordinary young man of no particular strength or skill, would be living in a faraway, untamed land.

He shivered. No turning back.

"Never mind all that searching," Elias said in answer to Jasper's comments. His voice was more slurred than ever, making Sam wonder just how much grog he'd drunk. "Finding a treasure isn't difficult at all—*if* one knows where to look." He grinned and winked broadly.

Jasper scowled. "Look, old man," he said. "I'm getting right weary of your endless hints and smirks. I don't believe you know anything of any treasure at all. And if you might be thinking of hanging from my coattails, you can stop it right now."

"What?" Elias stood suddenly, nearly overturning his

barrel. "I need no coattails of *yours*, Riggs. I shall be off enjoying my *true* treasure while you are still telling tall tales of your imaginary one."

"Take that back!" Jasper growled, grabbing Elias by the collar.

"I will not!" Elias cried.

"Easy, now," William said, rising to his feet. "Let's not come to blows, fellows."

Jasper ignored him, glaring into Elias's face instead. Sam, who was sitting near Elias, shrank back from the fury in the younger man's eyes.

"I am not the one who imagines treasure," Jasper spat. "You are all talk, old man. You know nothing of treasure— or anything else."

"Don't be so sure." Elias shoved him away. "What I have in my possession will lead me to—but never mind. It's no business of yours."

Jasper's face twisted with anger. "Why, you . . ."

"What's all this then?" a loud voice boomed, making them all jump.

Glancing around, Sam saw the ship's captain striding across the deck toward them. Captain Bradford walked as steadily as if he were marching through Covent Garden in London rather than on a pitching, rolling ship. Judging by the respect with which every man, woman, and child treated the stern, no-nonsense captain, Sam suspected that even the ship and the sea dared not upset him by sending him off balance. Under his disapproving gaze, Jasper slunk off in one direction, most of the others quickly following.

"Very well, then," Captain Bradford said to no one in particular. Spinning on his heel, he marched away.

Seeing that Elias was slumped on his barrel seat, Sam reached out to help him. "Come along," he said. "Let's get you off to bed."

"Many thanks, my lad," Elias said, leaning heavily on Sam's shoulder as they made their way to the passenger hold. "Perhaps I've had a drop too much this evening."

Soon the older man was lying wearily upon his straw pallet. Several other settlers were already snoring in their own corners, and the faint stench of vomit indicated that at least one of them had been troubled by the rough sea.

"All right, then?" Sam said as Elias closed his eyes. "I'm off to tuck in myself."

But he hesitated, still thinking about what he'd just

heard up on deck. He wondered if Jasper might be right. The portly, mild-mannered Elias certainly didn't *seem* like the type of man who was likely to strike it rich in the New World.

"Do you really believe you'll find treasure when we arrive?" Sam asked impulsively.

The older man's eyes opened and peered at Sam in the dim light of the hold. "I know it, son," Elias wheezed, struggling to a half-sitting position. "You seem a good sort of fellow. Head on right. Come closer—I can trust you, can't I?"

Sam nodded, holding his breath—partly through anticipation of what Elias might tell him, and partly to avoid the old man's breath, which was atrocious.

"It's like this, m'boy," Elias began in a low voice after looking around to be sure he wouldn't be overheard. "A few years back, my brother Isaac received a letter from a younger cousin of ours. A Cousin Gilbert. Gilbert traveled to Jamestown several years back—1607, to be precise."

"Part of Christopher Newport's original party?" Sam asked. "The men who founded Jamestown Settlement?"

Elias blinked at him, obviously impressed by Sam's

knowledge. "That's right," he said. "The exploring urge runs in our family. Gilbert went not only for the adventure and potential wealth, but also in search of our Great-Uncle James, who had settled at Roanoke Colony back in the 1580s and vanished along with all the rest of the settlers there."

Sam's eyes widened. He had heard tales all his life of the Lost Colony of Roanoke. It had been founded under the sponsorship of Sir Walter Raleigh, the well-known poet and explorer who was currently imprisoned in the Tower of London for plotting against the king. Raleigh had first tried to settle the Roanoke area in 1585, but that attempt had failed. The settlers had run into troubles with the native tribes and had returned to England the following year. Then, in 1587, some five years before Sam himself was born, Raleigh had sent the artist and gentleman, John White, to make a second attempt at colonizing the New World. White landed at the settlement that had been abandoned by an earlier group, along with more than one hundred men, women, and children. They revived the settlement, and there was even a baby born—Virginia Dare, the first English child born in the New World.

But, as Sam had read, once again there had been much

trouble with several of the unfriendly local tribes who had clashed with the earlier settlers, and well before a year had passed, White headed back to England in search of help. Then bad weather and the battle against the Spanish Armada had delayed his return voyage. When he finally did return to Roanoke in 1590, the settlers had vanished. There was no sign of struggle or attack, and the only clue was the name of a friendly local tribe—the Croatoan—carved into a tree. To this day, nobody knew what had become of those early settlers. Sam's father called it one of the great mysteries of modern times and had often engaged the entire family in speculation about it during Sam's boyhood.

Shaking his head clear of the memory, Sam focused on Elias. "Did Gilbert find any trace of your uncle?" he asked the older man curiously. "How near is Jamestown to Roanoke?"

Elias shrugged. "I do not know the answer to either question," he said, putting out a hand to steady himself as the ship pitched and rolled. "Gilbert had a coded note from him—or so he claimed. It was merely a scrap of parchment found at the settlement by one of the sailors and carried back to London on White's return journey." He shrugged and glanced around again. "Even Mr. White himself did not know of it—the sailor knew our family and brought it secretly back to Gilbert's father."

"What did the note say?" Sam's mind flashed to his own father, who enjoyed nothing more than a mysterious code.

"I do not know that either. I never saw it." Elias reached into the mess of belongings at the foot of his pallet. "But I did see this."

He pulled out a folded bit of paper. "Is that the letter from your cousin to your brother Isaac?" Sam guessed.

"Aye, my boy," Elias replied. "It urges Isaac and me to come to the New World ourselves, making cryptic reference to items of great value that may be found there. In it Gilbert indicates that he had hidden this treasure carefully, leaving a sign to show us the way in case anything happened to him before we arrived." Glancing down at the letter in his lap, Elias ran his stubby fingers over it in a practiced gesture— as if stroking a pup. "And it seems likely something did happen to him," he added. "We've heard nothing from him since this letter arrived some three years ago."

Sam could guess what the older man was thinking. Everyone in London had heard of the "Starving Time" that had struck the Jamestown Colony several winters earlier. The colony had already been troubled by drought and shipwrecks. When its leader, Captain John Smith, had been injured and forced to return to England, the local Powhatan tribe of natives had lost some of their trust in the settlers and become much more reluctant to trade with them. It was said that some four out of five settlers had been lost due to the food shortage that long winter. It was only the arrival of three supply ships commanded by Baron De La Warr that had saved the colony.

"If the letter arrived three years ago, why did it take so long for you to make this journey?" Sam asked. "And where is your brother Isaac? Why did he not come?"

"The answers to those two questions are connected," Elias said sadly. "Indeed, Isaac and I started planning our voyage immediately after we received the letter. But then Isaac was suddenly taken from us. The Black Death."

Sam shuddered, as every Englishman did, at the mention of that terrible scourge. He remembered the outbreak in 1608 that had closed the theaters in London, along with all other places of entertainment. It had killed four or five of the Gates family's neighbors, as well as his great aunt.

"After Isaac died, I forgot about the letter for a while," Elias went on, his voice growing heavy and sadder still. "Without clever Isaac, I figured there was little chance of finding the treasure. Besides that, it did not seem so important anymore. But after some time had passed, I found myself wondering again. I saw no reason not to look for Gilbert's treasure if there is one to be found. I am growing older, I have no wife or children who need me. What else have I to live for?"

Sam felt a flash of sympathy. Although their situations were vastly different, he thought he understood how Elias felt. Indeed, when faced with bleak prospects at home, why not try something new and exciting?

Elias ran a hand over his face, as if wiping away his sad thoughts. "In any case, I only hope I can decipher Cousin Gilbert's signs to find the treasure map. Isaac was always the one to enjoy codes and that sort of thing—when Gilbert was a boy, the two of them often traded secret notes and riddles."

"Might I have a look at the letter?" Sam asked. "My fath—uh, everyone says I have a clever mind for puzzles and such. If the letter holds a clue to the location of the treasure map, perhaps I can help you figure it out."

Elias unfolded the letter carefully and glanced down at it. "I suppose that would be all right," he says. "My feeble old mind might be needful of the help."

Sam took the letter from him. He began to scan the lines, but before reaching the end of the page there was a sudden outburst from outside the cabin. A second later William came in, laughing heartily with a couple of other passengers, one of whom had evidently been drunk enough to trip over the cannon on the way and knock out a tooth.

Quick as a wink, Elias grabbed the letter from Sam's hand and whisked it out of sight. "Don't tell a soul!" he whispered urgently.

Two

The next day dawned overcast and blustery. The *Susan Constant* creaked and moaned with each slap of the foam-tipped waves, and the crew clambered about in the rigging like monkeys, adjusting the sails. Sam had awakened earlier than most of the other passengers and crept out of the cabin, breathing in the fresh sea air out on deck. He had slept poorly, as he couldn't stop thinking about Elias's quest—and that letter. He had always been blessed with a superb memory. When he saw something once, whether book, play, or face, he rarely forgot even the slightest detail. In this case, he'd caught only the briefest glimpse of Elias's letter, but it had stuck.

Finding a private spot beside one of the cannons, he sat down, closed his eyes, and brought the image to mind. The ink had been faded, the paper spotted with moisture and age. But the words were still crisp and clean.

Dearest cousin, it had begun. *I trust this letter finds you and your brother well by the grace of God. I write this day to entreat the both of you to consider my humble recommendation to follow me here to this strange land which is indeed, as the rumors have it, a land of riches. I have myself stumbled upon something most interesting and of immense value, left here upon these new shores by our dear lost uncle, and in which I wish my favourite cousins to share. For this purpose I am sending you instructions and directions to find these items in case of any harm coming to myself in the meantime, though I dare not put the details of its location simply on paper because a mere Wax seal cannot hide such information from curious eyes. . . .*

Sam opened his eyes. That was the end of what he'd seen before Elias had snatched back the letter. There had been only a few more lines on the front of the page, though he'd seen no signature at the bottom, which he took to mean that the letter continued on the back.

Still, he had seen enough to wonder just how useful Elias's secret letter really was. Gilbert had stated plainly that he didn't dare put the location of his hidden treasure in the letter. How then were the brothers intended to find it?

Perhaps some clue leading to a map—if not the treasure itself—lies in the latter section, he told himself hopefully. *After all, Elias seems completely convinced he holds the key to finding those riches Gilbert mentions. Once he has slept off his grog, I shall see if I can find a private moment to get another look at that letter.*

In the meantime, he pulled out the pad of smooth, clean paper he had carried everywhere since his journey had begun. The tablet had been a bon voyage gift from Mr. Wesley, the owner of the bookbinder's shop where Sam had worked, and it was one of the loveliest and most valuable items Sam owned. Until now, he'd found nothing worthy of soiling the purity of its creamy pages.

He quickly wrote down all he could recall of the letter. A few minutes later he was still staring at the words, trying to figure out if he'd missed anything in the innocent-sounding lines, when he heard heavy footsteps rapidly approaching across the creaky wooden deck. He glanced up just in time to see William and Jasper round the cannon and come to a stop before him.

"There you are, baby brother," William said. "I was beginning to think you'd gone overboard."

Jasper chuckled and slapped William on the back in a friendly way. "We can't have that! Lucky we found him."

Sam narrowed his eyes. Why were William and Jasper treating each other as such great friends? They'd never acted so close before.

"What do you have there, young Samuel?" Jasper asked

in a jocular tone. "Making notes of our journey, like Captain John Smith or some such fellow?" He winked. "Or perhaps are you working on a treasure map? Did that old drunk Turner give you any hints last night, eh?"

Suddenly, Sam understood Jasper's friendly mood. Climbing to his feet, he tucked his notebook away out of sight.

"If you're hoping I will betray Elias's secrets, you might as well give it up," he said, too annoyed to temper his words. "I know little more than you do of the supposed treasure."

William chuckled, but Jasper's affable expression wavered. His thin lips twisted into a grimace, and he looked Sam up and down.

"All right, I see you are a plainspoken sort," he said. All traces of good humor were gone, replaced by grim resolve. "So let us be plain with one another then. Thus far I have assumed Turner to be nothing but a batty old fool. But he made reference last night to something in his possession that would lead him to treasure, and that makes me think he may have a map after all. There's no telling if it is real, but I wish to find out. And I figure you boys can help me." He glanced at William, then back at Sam again.

"What do you mean?" William asked, furrowing his brow in confusion. "You think old Elias really has a map showing how to find this Treasure of the Ancients?"

"Perhaps, or perhaps not." Jasper rubbed his narrow chin and shot a suspicious glance around the deck. The sun was rising overhead, and more of the passengers were out and about. "But if there is treasure to be found with his map, I think *we* should be the ones to find it."

Sam didn't bother to correct Jasper's impression that Elias's clue was a map. After all, if the letter did hold some sort of clue in its final lines, it added up to the same thing.

"Sounds like a fair offer," William said, smiling and clapping Jasper on the back. "And the good Lord knows we could use a bit of treasure these days, eh, Sam?"

"That much is true," Sam admitted. For a moment he allowed himself to imagine it—he and William would go into partnership with Jasper. True, William wouldn't be much help in figuring out the clues, but Jasper seemed a cunning sort, and between him and Sam, surely they could puzzle it out. William's brawn would come in handy later for digging up the treasure and hauling the gold and jewels away. Once the treasure was theirs, there would be no need to eke out a backbreaking living in the new colony. He and William could return to London immediately, pay off their father's debts, and proceed to show everyone what a successful Gates looked like. . . .

"Well?" Jasper was watching Sam carefully, his blood-shot blue eyes glittering in his thin, sun-reddened face. "Do we have a deal, men?"

"No," Sam said firmly before William could answer. "I won't betray Elias. It is his treasure to seek, not yours, Jasper."

"But, Sam . . ." William began, sounding surprised.

"Do not decide this in haste, young friend." Jasper's tone remained silky smooth and calm, but it held the distinct hint of a threat. "I am offering you a share in my success, and I don't make that offer lightly. *Or* take kindly to having my largesse refused."

Sam felt his stomach lurch with unease. He had never been one to seek out conflict and, in fact, tended to shrink away from it whenever possible. Still, despite the barely veiled threat, he held Jasper's gaze.

"I know exactly what you are offering," Sam said. "And you already have my answer."

Jasper swore under his breath. "Very well," he replied, his voice icy. "I thought you were a sensible fellow, young Mr. Gates. Clearly I was wrong."

"Come, now," William said soothingly. "Perhaps we can discuss this together like rational men?"

"Sadly, it seems I must be the one to tell you that your brother is no man, Gates," Jasper spat out. "He is not even a boy, for boys do grow into men eventually. No, he might as well be made of—of wax. For he melts like a candle at the least sign of adversity." He glowered at Sam. "I think you might find that tendency a very serious problem once we arrive in Jamestown."

William drew himself up to his full height, his broad face growing red. "Is that meant to be a threat against my brother, Mr. Riggs?" he demanded, his immense hands clenching into fists at his sides. "I'll thank you to be off now, before you say something I shall have to make you regret."

Sam hardly noticed as Jasper and William traded a few more barbs before Jasper backed down, clearly not wanting to a fight a man as imposing as William. Soon, Jasper went slinking off across the deck, muttering darkly to himself.

As the treasure hunter disappeared from sight, his nasty words lingered in Sam's mind, though not in the insulting way they'd been intended.

Made of wax, he thought, excitement flaring up in him like a freshly trimmed and lit candle. *Wax . . .*

Three

Elias was sitting upon his pallet yawning and scratching his beard when Sam found him a short while later. The hold area was otherwise deserted—on a mild day, few passengers cared to spend any more time than necessary in the stuffy, crowded, smelly area belowdecks, where the odors of the unwashed people who slept there mingled with the stench wafting up through the floorboards from the livestock hold just below.

"Samuel, my boy." Elias yawned again and rubbed the top of his head, making his gray hair stand on end. "I do believe I've slept off most of the grog I drank last night."

"I'm glad of that. But listen, Elias." Sam's excitement had only grown since his earlier brainstorm. "I just remembered something—wasn't the word 'wax' capitalized in Gilbert's letter?"

Elias blinked, looking confused. "Eh?"

"The letter," Sam insisted. "Please—can you check? I want to be certain I'm remembering it right."

"You are," Elias said, not moving from his spot except

to reach around and scratch his backside. "I believe 'wax' is indeed capitalized. But what of it?"

"I just found myself wondering why he would do that," Sam said, growing more excited. "Some people capitalize lots of words in all their writing, of course, but Gilbert only did it with that one that I noted. It must mean something, mustn't it? He clearly wanted to emphasize that word, that seemingly innocuous little word. Wax—what could it mean? Perhaps the treasure map is hidden beneath a candle somewhere in Jamestown, or even carved right into one!" He shrugged. "True, it is a bit tricky and obscure, perhaps, but maybe . . . ?"

Elias was finally starting to look a bit more awake. "By Jove, you could be right!" he said. "I've never given it much thought. But that *does* sound like something Gilbert might have come up with. And something he might have expected Isaac to figure out." He smiled, his eyes going distant. "Those two with their little codes and such—"

"That must be it, then," Sam said, not giving Elias a chance to finish. "The letter holds the code to finding the treasure map!"

Elias's smile faded, replaced by a sad look. "Yes," he

said. "A code meant for Isaac. I'm certain that Gilbert meant for him to interpret his clues, and wanted me along only to help with the heavy lifting. And now there's just me. . . ."

Sam smiled uncomfortably, reminded of his thoughts about himself and William during the conversation with Jasper. But he pushed that aside.

"Listen," he told Elias. "As I told you, I'm good at puzzles and things just like your brother was. When I was younger, my father used to challenge me with codes and ask me to try to put together tricky bits of clock parts. And I was already beating my elders at chess and whist while most boys my age were still playing with tops. Perhaps I can help you break the code!"

Elias shrugged, still wearing a pessimistic expression. "Perhaps," he said. "But so far your code breaking seems to have gotten us nowhere, my young friend. If the map was any part of a beeswax candle three years ago, there's little chance it would still be in existence after so much time."

Sam's heart sank as he realized the older man was right. Still, he couldn't quite give up hope. Figuring out that first possible clue had whetted his appetite for more.

"Might I see the letter again?" he asked. "I didn't get to finish reading it last night."

"Of course." Elias dug into his possessions. As he did so, he let out a curse.

"What is it?" Sam's heart nearly stopped. What if Jasper had sneaked over to Elias's pallet during the night and stolen the letter?

But a second later Elias's hand came free, with the letter clutched in it. "Forgive my language, young man," he said with a laugh. "I caught my ring on my spare breeches and feared I'd ripped them."

Sam glanced at the heavy gold ring that Elias wore on his left hand. He'd noticed it before—the long journey and cramped quarters had given him opportunity enough to notice every hair on every mole belonging to his fellow passengers—but he hadn't thought much of it. But now that he took a closer look, he saw for the first time that it had an odd picture etched into its face. It appeared to be a human eye surrounded by lines.

"What is that symbol on your ring?" he asked. "Is it supposed to be an eye?"

"I believe so, yes." Elias held out his hand so that it was

illuminated by a beam of watery sunlight coming through from above. "This ring was my brother's," he said. "Isaac was a stonemason and a loyal member of his craftsman's lodge. The symbol is theirs."

"Oh." Sam had heard of such freemasons' lodges from his father, who admired the members' fine craftsmanship.

"Isaac was never seen without this ring," Elias went on. "He wore it proudly every day of his life. When he died, I took it to remember him by." He touched the ring briefly with the opposite finger. When he spoke again his voice was husky. "Whether or not we find treasure in the New World, it will always be my most valued possession."

Sam looked away, giving the older man a chance to compose himself. Now he was doubly glad that he hadn't given in to the temptation of Jasper's offer. Finding this treasure was clearly about more than gold and riches to Elias. His quest in the New World was a way for him to remember his brother and cousin—and perhaps to help revive the fortune and reputation of his family. And that was a purpose with which Sam could certainly sympathize.

After a moment Elias cleared his throat and sat up a bit straighter. "You wanted to see the letter again, my boy?"

"Oh—yes." Sam reached over and took it from him. Opening it carefully, he crouched down and smoothed it out across his lap, taking advantage of the weak sunbeam from above.

This time he was able to read the letter straight through without interruption. He skimmed past the earlier part quickly, then lingered over the remaining words.

Dearest cousin,

I trust this letter finds you and your brother well by the grace of God. I write this day to entreat the both of you to consider my humble recommendation to follow me here to this strange land which is indeed, as the rumors have it, a land of riches. I have myself stumbled upon something most interesting and of immense value, left here upon these new shores by our dear lost uncle, and in which I wish my favourite cousins to share.

For this purpose I am sending you instructions and directions to find these items in case of any harm coming to myself in the meantime, though I dare not put the details of its location simply on paper because a mere Wax seal cannot hide such information from curious eyes as may be about.

Please arrange passage with as much haste as you can. God per-

mitting, I shall soon be greeting you and elias on the shores of this new land. If that is not to be, it is my only hope that this letter has shed enough Light on the matter for you to go on without me. Otherwise these items shall remain as lost as the man who left them for me years ago.

However, I am confident that you can prevail, should you only maintain a true and Constant heart.

Your cousin always,
Gilbert

Four

The sunbeam faded, blocked by the clouds. But Sam stared at the letter in the near dark, puzzling over the remaining lines.

"See anything, my boy?" Elias asked.

Sam rubbed his chin. "Nothing very clear," he said. "But I still find the capitalization odd. See here—he does not even capitalize your name." He pointed to the spot. "Yet aside from the Lord's name, there are three other words that *are* capitalized. Wax, Light, and Constant." He glanced up at Elias, who was peering at the letter over his shoulder. "Constant—like the name of our very ship, the *Susan Constant*. Do you know if Gilbert traveled to the New World on this ship? Or was he aboard one of the other two?"

Elias shrugged. "I have no idea," he said. "Are you sure the word *Constant* is not mere coincidence? If it were only one word thus oddly capitalized, it would indeed seem a clue. But three?"

"I suppose it could be a coincidence." Sam returned his gaze to the spidery handwriting before him. He couldn't shake the feeling that there was a clue there somewhere if only he could decipher it. "But what if I am right? What if your cousin was on the *Constant*'s earlier voyage, and is now referring to it as some sort of clue?"

"I do not see how that could be." Elias tugged on one protruding ear, still sounding dubious. "What would the ship have to do with the treasure? Gilbert could not have hidden a map on board—he discovered the treasure once he had landed, and the ship would surely have been away again by then."

"Yes, you are right about that," Sam said slowly. But those odd capitalizations were still tickling something in his brain. "There must be some meaning there—"

He cut himself off, hearing a sudden creak of the floorboards from close by. Looking up from the letter, he gasped as he saw that Jasper was in the sleeping area just a few paces away. He had crept in as silently as a cat, but a loose bit of wood had given him away.

Elias spotted him, too, and whisked the letter out of sight. Jasper chuckled and stepped closer.

"Looking over your treasure map, old man?" he asked. "Do not worry; I have not come to steal it from you. I am seeking your young friend there." He nodded toward Sam.

"You have found me. Now what is it you want with me?" Sam asked, trying not to let his voice betray his nervousness. What if Jasper did want to snatch the letter, which he still clearly assumed was a treasure map? Would he and Elias be able to stop him, even with two against one?

But Jasper, who was still relaxed and smiling, made no move to approach Elias. "I have come to offer my apology, Samuel," he said. "My earlier outburst against you was unwarranted. I do hope you shall find it in you to forgive me this once?"

"Er, there is no need of apology." Sam wondered if William had beaten this sudden contrition into Jasper. "I had forgotten it already."

"Good, good." Jasper stretched out his hand. "We are friends again, then, lad?"

Sam cautiously took his hand and shook it. "Friend" was not a word he would ever choose to apply to Jasper, but he did not think it prudent to say so.

"My feelings toward you remain unchanged," he said instead.

Elias started to rise heavily to his feet, looking confused.

"Did you two have a disagreement?"

"Nothing serious." Jasper reached out to help him up. "Now come—the weather is poor today, and I find myself in need of some grog to make the sun seem brighter. Care to join me, gentlemen?"

"I think I just might, now that you mention it," Elias agreed. "A nip or two might chase away this headache of mine."

"Thanks, but I'd better go see what William is up to," Sam said.

"Suit yourself," Jasper said with a chuckle. "More for us then, eh, Turner?"

Elias laughed. "Quite right, my friend! Quite right."

"Come, then." Jasper smiled, stepped back, and held out a hand to allow the older man to pass out of the hold in front of him.

But when Elias's back was to him, Jasper's smile faded instantly. And the look he shot the older man chilled Sam to the bone.

That night Sam sat bolt upright from a deep sleep. The ship was pitching and creaking as rain lashed at the sails, and the distant shouts of the crew and the much closer moans of seasick passengers were swallowed in the rumbles of thunder that shook the ship from bow to stern. From the lower hold came the thumps of the cattle and pigs and the bleating of frightened sheep.

But it was neither the storm nor the animals that had awakened Sam. Rather, it was a dream. "That's it," he said to himself, his mind filled with images of clocks.

He had been dreaming he was back home in London. Instead of working at the bookbinder's shop, he was apprenticed to Elias, who was a clockmaker like Sam's own father.

"See here," Dream Elias had told him, holding up a mess of clock parts. "Each bit of the clock causes the next element to move. You cannot get this one to work until that one is in place. And then we add this one, and then this . . ."

In the dream, Sam had refused to accept what Elias was saying. He had tried again and again to read the time from the clock he was holding. But it was no use, for the clock was missing half its parts, including the hour hand.

"It must mean something," Dream Sam had insisted stubbornly, shaking the useless clock. "It must mean something."

Now, Waking Sam sat in the darkness swaying with the

motion of the ship. *It does mean something,* he told himself. *Perhaps the clue in the letter isn't pointing us toward the treasure map after all. It could merely be guiding us to the next clue for finding such a map!*

He rolled over on his pallet, searching by feel for his belongings. Finally his hand closed over the smooth surface of his writing tablet. A flash of lightning illuminated the hold, showing him the path between his fellow passengers. Moments later he was on the lower deck just outside the hold, huddled against the base of the main mast to shelter himself from the worst of the driving rain. He opened his notebook and read over the letter, which he had inscribed there in full the day before, by the light of a sputtering lantern nearby.

Wax, he thought, his gaze lingering as always over those odd, seemingly random capitalizations. *Light. Constant.*

He smiled, not even noticing as a sudden change in the wind dashed cold rain against his face and extinguished the lantern. That was it!

Glancing back into the cavelike interior of the hold, he wished he could talk over his idea with Elias right away. But the older man had spent much of the previous day and well into the evening carousing with Jasper. It would do no good to try to rouse him until he had fully recovered.

With an impatient sigh, Sam crawled back into the hold. He lay awake for some time, listening to the storm and thinking about his theory. But finally, as the roiling waves subsided and thunder vibrated through the ship less frequently, he fell into a restless sleep.

"Elias?" Sam shook the older man by the shoulder. "Elias, wake up!"

The bright morning sun was shining in through the entryway, and the ship rocked peacefully on gentle waves, all traces of the previous night's storm gone. After tossing and turning for hours, Sam had finally fallen more deeply asleep and awakened only after the sun was well up and the rest of the passengers had left the hold. All except one passenger, that was—Elias was huddled in his blanket at the far end of the sleeping area.

At Sam's touch, the older man let out a low groan and shifted slightly. But his eyes remained closed.

"Samuel?" he croaked out. "Is that you?"

"Yes, it's me." Looking at Elias's pale face, Sam couldn't help but wonder just how much grog Elias had put away the day before. "Time to get up. I wish to speak with you about something."

For a long moment Elias didn't respond. Finally letting out a long, rattling breath, he cracked one eye open. It looked bloodshot and weary.

"I think it shall have to wait, m'boy," he mumbled. "I'm not feeling myself this morning."

"All right." Sam did his best to hide his impatience. "I shall be back a little later then."

But when he checked on Elias an hour later, he found him much the same. And once another hour had passed with no change for the better, he grew worried.

"Are you sick?" he asked. "Shall I fetch the captain?"

"Do not bother the captain on my account," Elias wheezed, his words barely comprehensible.

Sam rocked back on his heels, biting his lip as he gazed down at the older man. Elias looked terrible. His skin was gray and drawn except for his cheeks, which burned bright pink. His limbs trembled with every effort to move. And a foul stench came from his mouth with each breath.

"I'm going to alert the captain," Sam announced. He waited a moment, but there was no response from Elias.

Moments later, Sam found Captain Bradford near the foremast and told him of Elias's condition. The captain seemed concerned and promised to send someone to look at him immediately.

Sam lingered a moment, wanting to say something else. The captain raised a stern eyebrow at him.

"That will be all, lad," he said in a voice that allowed no argument. "Be off with you now."

"All right. Thank you, Captain." Sam wandered away and found William playing All Fours with another passenger on the cannon deck.

"What's the matter with you?" William asked, lowering his cards when he got a look at Sam's face.

"It's Elias," Sam said. "He's not well."

William laughed. "That's what comes of drinking all day and night, brother. Let it be a lesson to you."

Another hour had passed when a sailor approached Sam, who was standing at the stern staring out at the ship's wake. The weather had turned cloudy again, and a cold rain was starting to mix with the sea spray.

"The sick man has asked for you, mate," the sailor said. "Best hurry—methinks the reaper may be coming soon for that one. Let us hope it's not catching."

His heart in his throat, Sam hurried to the hold. The sailor hadn't exaggerated—Elias looked much worse than before. He was awake now, though still curled on his pallet. Fresh vomit tinged with blood puddled on the floor beside him, and his body was wracked by spasms of coughing.

"My boy," Elias croaked out, his bleary eyes focusing as Sam kneeled beside him. "Come closer. I have something to say, and I wish no one else to hear."

Sam glanced around. The worsening weather outside was chasing many of the passengers back into the hold, though most needed no more than a glance at Elias's condition to give him a wide berth.

"What is it, Elias?" Sam said, leaning closer.

"I do believe I'm about to die, my lad." Elias's voice was hoarse and low, but his words were clearer than they'd been all day.

"No!" Sam blurted out. "You'll be all right, Elias. You just need to sleep a while, and you'll be good as new."

"Oh, I'll be sleeping soon enough, I wager." Elias let out a short laugh that quickly turned into another spasm of wracking coughs. It was a moment or two before he was able to speak again. "No, this is it for me. But before it's too late, I wanted you to have a couple of things."

He reached under his blanket and pulled out the letter, pressing it into Sam's hand. Then he took his other hand and pressed something small and cold into it.

Sam looked down at it. "Isaac's ring?" he said. "But . . ."

"I want you to have it," Elias rasped. "Isaac would be pleased to know that it made it to the New World, even if neither of us did."

His voice trailed off, and his breath gave a strange hitch and rattle. "Elias?" Sam said tentatively. "Elias!"

But there was no answer. Elias was gone.

Sam blinked back a few tears, then slipped on the ring. It was far too loose on his finger, so he strung it on a bit of leather and hung it around his neck instead, then tucked the letter away in his clothes. He stared around the sleeping hold, not knowing what to do next. His head was spinning with the swiftness of his friend's demise. Even the black death didn't take people quite so quickly. . . .

He searched the gloomy hold for Jasper's narrow face, but it was nowhere to be seen. William was not there, either. Spotting a kind-faced, motherly woman known as Mary, he went to her and told her what had happened. She bustled over to Elias's body, along with a couple of other women. Soon a young boy was dispatched to fetch the captain, and Sam backed away, feeling unneeded.

Heading out of the hold, he found that it was raining in earnest now, a gray, steady downpour that promised to go on for a long while. No one was on deck except for a sailor high up in the rigging and a couple more working the ropes and shouting to each other at the main mast. Sam was soaked to the skin within moments, but he paid no attention as he headed up to the forecastle and started pacing back and forth, thinking about what had happened.

Could it be a coincidence that Elias had fallen mortally ill immediately after spending time with Jasper? He looked out over the fretful sea. And even if Jasper *was* responsible for Elias's death, what could Sam do about it? He had no proof, no way to convince anyone of Jasper's motive without revealing Elias's secret. . . .

Suddenly, rough hands grabbed him. Sam let out a shout and struggled furiously, but it was no use. A second later he was dangling over the edge of the ship looking straight down into the rough Atlantic waters.

"Hey!" he blurted out, trying to twist around to see who was holding him. "Let me go!"

"Are you *certain* that's what you want?" a voice purred in response.

Sam gulped as he recognized the voice—Jasper's—and realized its meaning. He stared, transfixed, as a stormy wave crashed against the side of the ship with an explosion of foam that splashed his face.

"Now, then," Jasper said, his voice barely loud enough to be heard over the driving rain and pounding sea. "I'd like you to hand over that treasure map, young Gates. Otherwise I trust you're in the mood for a swim."

Five

Sam was frozen with terror. Part of him was ready to rip the letter from its hiding place and hand it over. Then again, what guarantee was there that Jasper wouldn't drop him into the sea anyway?

Before he could decide what to do, he heard a shout. A split-second later another pair of strong hands grabbed him by the collar and hauled him back over the edge, dropping him onto the deck with a thud.

"What's the meaning of this?" William's shout was a fearsome thing to hear, making even Jasper cower. "That is my brother!"

Sam went limp as he realized he'd been saved. Jasper was backing rapidly away from William, looking nervous.

"Easy, Gates," he said. "Let's not do anything we'll regret. . . ."

"Trust me, I shall not regret this at all." Striding forward, William swung his massive fist. It connected with Jasper's jaw with a solid *thwunk!*

Jasper cried out and staggered back. William pressed his advantage, landing several more punches until Jasper finally went down, sprawling on the deck with blood pouring out of his nose and a cut on his cheek. Several other passengers had come on deck and noticed what was going on.

A sailor heard the commotion, too, and swung down from the rigging. "Enough, men!" he shouted. "Let's be done with this foolishness, or I'll have to fetch the captain."

"All right." William gave Jasper one last kick in the ribs. "I trust this will remind you not to bother my brother again, Riggs."

Jasper scrambled to his feet without answering. He glared from Sam to William, the rain sending bloody rivulets down his face and shirt. Then he limped off and disappeared.

"You all right, brother?" William reached down and pulled Sam to his feet as the sailor and other spectators drifted off in search of drier ground. "What was that all about, anyway?"

"It's a long story." Sam was still a bit breathless from his close call with death. Clearly, Jasper believed that Elias's treasure was worth murdering for, which made it all the more likely that he'd been behind the older man's sudden passing. And now Sam was the one with the only clue!

A pounding from William won't put him off for long, he realized, touching both ring and letter to be sure they were still with him. *He'll be back for more as soon as he sees the opportunity.*

He shuddered at the thought. Maybe it would be best to give in, to find Jasper and give him the map before he had the chance to try again. . . .

Then again, he'd joined this expedition for adventure. Was he going to show himself a coward, now that adventure had found him?

No, he told himself firmly. *By the Gates name, I shall not!*

"Sammy?" William said. "Are you all right? Your face has a funny look."

"I need your help," Sam blurted out. "Can you create a distraction for a while?"

"A distraction?" William looked confused as he peered at Sam through the rain. "What do you mean? Why?"

Sam took a deep breath. "Because I'm going to break into Captain Bradford's cabin."

"What?" William exclaimed. "What would possess you to do such a thing?"

"I don't have time to explain," Sam said. "But I'll tell you everything later, I swear it. For now, I just need something that will keep everyone away from that part of the ship. Can you help me, William?"

William hesitated. "I do not understand you, little brother." He rubbed his chin, his eyes taking on a sly glint. "But can I help you?" he added. "You know I can."

Sam grinned at him. He had suspected and hoped that it wouldn't take much to convince William to go along with his plan. He was always up for a bit of mischief.

After a brief discussion, William hurried off toward the hold while Sam headed in the other direction. Now that the plan was in motion, he was already wondering if it might not be too risky. His steps came more and more slowly as he neared the captain's cabin at one end of the main deck. The door was closed, and there was no sound from within. Sam leaned against a large coil of rope a few feet from the door, feeling nervous and conspicuous.

What will the captain do if he catches me in there? he wondered with a shudder. *This is never going to work. . . .*

But it *had* to work. Sam knew that his plan was desperate, but the ship would be reaching the New World within a matter of weeks, if not days. He had to take his chance when he could find it. And if his hunch about the letter was correct, that meant getting a look around the captain's cabin.

The rain had slowed by now, but there was still little sign of life on deck. Even the few sailors visible at the moment were busy at the other end of the ship. And surely Captain Bradford was still dealing with Elias's body. That meant there was nobody near enough to notice if Sam were to slip inside the cabin right now, without waiting for William's distraction. . . .

He knew he should wait, play it safe. But he was afraid that if he stood there any longer, he might lose his nerve. His heart thumping and the blood racing in his veins, he scurried over, pushed the door open, and slipped inside.

The cabin was gloomy, the single window providing barely enough rain-dimmed daylight to see one's hand in front of one's face. Sam squinted, trying to make out the details of the place. The captain's small, neat bunk was set along one wall. Most of the other wall space was taken up by shelves holding nautical instruments, and the rest of the room was filled by a small, plain wooden table where several maps were held down by a sturdy metal lantern.

As Sam's eyes adjusted to the dark, the objects on the shelves came into focus. He searched through them, trying not to disturb anything, and soon found a wooden box of beeswax candles.

His heart thumping anew, he pulled the box from its shelf, nearly knocking over a large compass in the process. Squatting on the floor, he opened the candle box and dumped out its contents. At that moment the ship hit a swell and pitched to one side, sending most of the candles rolling off under the table.

Sam leaped after them, scrabbling desperately to gather them up again. He grabbed the last one just in time to stop it falling into a crack on the floor. Whew! Candles were expensive; if any went missing, the captain would surely be suspicious. . . .

Trying not to think about that, he sat on the floor with the candles in his lap. He picked up the box they'd been in and examined it. The box was made of wood and very plain; only the words "beeswax candles" and "London" and a crude drawing of a flame marked its top. There was no clue in any of that as far as Sam could see.

He next turned his attention to the candles themselves.

Picking them up one by one and squinting at them as best he could in the shadowy darkness, he tried to see if there was anything unusual about any of them.

Finally he gave up and shoved them all back in the box. *What use was this, anyway?* he wondered hopelessly. There was little chance that the same box of candles would remain here from the time of Gilbert's passage until now. And surely Gilbert himself would have realized that.

He sat back on his heels for a moment, staring blankly into space and thinking hard. This could be his only chance in the captain's cabin. If there was a clue to be found here, he had to find it now.

As he stood to return the box to its spot, he bumped hard against the corner of the wooden table, setting its contents to rattling. Pain flared in Sam's hip where it had made contact, but he hardly noticed. He was staring at the lantern rocking back and forth on the table. On first glimpse he'd taken it for an oil lantern, but now he saw that it was more like an elaborate candle holder with several wax candles within. The metal exterior was battered and darkened with age; it looked as if it had survived more than a few years at sea.

Of course! he thought, hope flaring once again. Hurriedly

shoving the box back onto its shelf, he grabbed the lantern, which sent the maps slipping around with every slight roll of the ship.

The lantern was heavy. Sam lifted it up, peering at it closely. The top part was decorated with etched waves and sea creatures, and there were a couple of lines of script engraved around the base.

Sam's heart let out another thump. Wax . . . Light . . . the heart of the *Constant*. Could this be it? Could Gilbert have been referring to the words on this ship's candle lantern in his letter?

He ran his finger over the engraving, squinting as hard as he could. But it was no use. The metal was dark with age, and combined with the cabin's dimness, it was impossible to make out the words.

Sam glanced over his shoulder at the box of candles. If he lit one, there was a risk that someone might see it through the window. But perhaps it was worth it. . . .

Before he could reach a decision, the sound of heavy footsteps broke into his thoughts. Along with the footsteps came voices—and they were coming from just outside!

". . . 'tis a shame, that—I dislike losing a passenger for

any reason," Captain Bradford's booming voice drifted in, barely muffled by the door. "But never mind, life goes on, eh? Now come inside and I'll show you that chart."

"Aye, Captain," the first mate's voice replied.

Sam froze, still clutching the lantern in both hands. He glanced around frantically for a way out. But the window was far too small to wriggle through, and if he tried to hide in the bunk or beneath the table, he would be spotted immediately.

He was trapped!

Six

Sam could do nothing but stand there, transfixed, as the door slowly swung inward. His mind raced trying to come up with a story that might explain his presence to the captain. But he could imagine nothing that would excuse him, even if he were somehow able to stammer it out before the captain hauled him off to the brig.

At that very moment, a chorus of shouts rang out from somewhere farther away.

"What's that?" the captain exclaimed from outside. "Sounds as if something is going on belowdecks."

Before the first mate could respond, the sounds of squealing pigs and bleating sheep rose above the continuing shouts. "All hands!" a voice drifted from somewhere toward the center of the ship. "The livestock are loose!"

The captain muttered an oath, and the door swung shut again. Then came the sound of footsteps racing off in the direction of the hold.

Sam went limp with relief. William's distraction had

come just in time. Just as the brothers had planned earlier, he must have sneaked down, set the livestock free from their pens in the lower hold, and spooked them into a frenzy before raising the alarm. The entire ship would be busy for quite some time trying to round up the creatures again.

That meant Sam had a few moments, at least, with no danger of being spotted. Rather than wasting time lighting a candle, he opened the door and stepped outside. To his relief, the rain had all but stopped, and there was more than enough sunlight filtering through the watery clouds for him to make out the crusty old lantern's inscription:

Those lost leave their mark
Hail the Crown, heed the dark.
—White, 1590

≈ ≈

"**L**and ho!"

At the sailor's cry, Sam rushed to the front of the ship with the rest of the passengers on deck. Sure enough, a dark, blurry smudge on the horizon now broke the endless blue sea that was all they'd seen for weeks, showing that they were nearing journey's end at last. The rest of the passengers began chattering excitedly but Sam remained silent, staring, with mixed feelings, at the distant line of land. In the week and a half that had passed since finding the message on the lantern, he had come no closer to figuring out the clue.

If it is a real clue at all, he thought, not for the first time. *It's quite possible that Cousin Gilbert might have seen that lantern on his initial voyage to Jamestown five years ago and remembered the inscription. But even if he did, what does it mean? Does it mean anything? Or is this all just my own crazy imaginings based on Elias's wild stories? William has always said that seeing all those plays would poison my mind with strange and dangerous ideas. . . .*

He shivered as he noticed Jasper talking with another passenger nearby. Sam had managed to avoid being alone with the treasure hunter since their last confrontation—not too difficult a task on the cramped, overcrowded vessel. Still, he could tell by the evil looks Jasper shot him now and then that the older man hadn't forgotten their unfinished business.

Just then, William strode over and clapped him on the shoulder so hard that Sam staggered a half step forward. "How about that, eh, little brother?" he exclaimed. "Land!

Looks like we'll finally be getting off this waterlogged prison. Now the real adventure starts!"

"Yes." Sam touched Isaac's ring through his shirt. He still hadn't told his brother about the letter's hidden clue. It had been easy enough to put him off with a made-up story about breaking into the captain's cabin to find a lost button. He'd felt guilty about the lie but figured it was better that way. If William knew about the treasure, it would make him Jasper's target as well. Besides, William had no patience for riddles and puzzles—he would be no help at all in figuring out the clue even if he were in on the secret.

I wish Elias was here, Sam thought, sadness coursing through him. *Maybe with his help I'd be able to figure it out.*

Once again, he turned over the words on the candle-holder in his mind. He'd written the phrase down in his notebook immediately, of course, though there was really no need—the words were emblazoned on his mind. He had thought of little else for the past ten days.

He was still pondering the problem some hours later when the ship entered the shallower waters at the mouth of a large river—the James, the captain told them all. At that point he forgot about the riddle for a while as he took in the strange new world that lay before him.

The teeming streets of London were all Sam had ever known, and even the vivid descriptions he'd read in books written by earlier explorers like Captain Smith and Lord De La Warr hadn't prepared him for this New World. Crowding the shoreline were trees—endless trees, more trees than Sam had seen in his life thus far, tall and wild and lush as no tree in London. Until then, Sam hadn't known there were so many trees in all the world as he saw now before him on the shores of Virginia. It was as if a gentleman's fine London garden had escaped the bounds of its brick walls, growing and growing out of control until nothing was left of walls, house, inhabitants . . . and then had continued growing, taking over city street, building, and everything else until all that was left in the world was an infinite expanse of foliage. And after so many weeks of dull blue and gray at sea, the tremendous canopy of green looked all the more vivid.

He pulled out his notebook and jotted down some of these thoughts. After that he kept his eyes on the shore as the ship passed from the deep blue of the sea into the murkier grayish water of the river. The trees that had seemed so still and monolithic from far off showed much more variety and movement on closer view—Sam saw branches waving in the breeze, birds flitting here and there, and once he thought he spotted a flash of movement nearer the ground, like something large moving quickly through the forest.

Red was standing beside him at that moment and let out a gasp. "Did you see that? Might've been the naturals! Hope they don't shoot at us with their arrows."

"Perhaps. Or it could have been a wild animal," Sam replied.

Red let out a laugh. "What's the difference? They're all equally savage from what I've heard."

Sam had heard plenty of stories about the native people of this new land, too. Most people said they were even more ruthless than the Spanish and killed English settlers every chance they got, but some accounts seemed to disagree.

"I've read Captain John Smith's book, *A True Relation of Such Occurrences and Accidents of Note as Happened in Virginia*," he told Red. "He wrote much of the native Powhatan tribes, including how he was befriended by their king's young daughter Pocahontas. Also there was much about trade with them and such. I wonder if they're really as savage as people say."

"I don't know." Red looked skeptical. "But I tell you, I'll not turn my back on any savage for fear of those arrows."

Sam shrugged. He figured he'd have firsthand experience of the savages soon enough. In any case, he doubted the natives' weapons would be any match for the *Constant*'s cannons if it came to that.

He stayed at the rail as the ship made its careful progress along the river. The crew dropped anchor in deep water soon after coming within sight of the wooden palisades of Fort James. Sam grabbed a rope for balance and stared out at what would be his new home. The cleared area around the fort's triangular walls was a violent brown gash in the otherwise unbroken soft green pelt of foliage that stretched away in every direction. A sailor let off shots from a caliver, and at the signal, dozens of people rushed out of the fort and down to the water's edge, waving and calling out to the ship and launching small boats to help ferry cargo and passengers ashore.

Soon, Sam found himself on dry land. It felt strange to step on solid ground after weeks at sea. For a while Sam continued to brace himself against pitches and swells that no longer came. By the way some of his fellow passengers staggered about, he guessed they were all having trouble shaking off their sea legs.

Captain Bradford, however, had no such trouble. Jumping out of his longboat, he strode confidently forward to greet the man at the front of the crowd that had gathered to greet the ship. The two men conferred privately for a moment.

Then the second man turned to address the ship's passengers. "Greetings, fair voyagers from the *Susan Constant*," he said in a rather pompous tone. "I wish to welcome you to the settlement of Jamestown on behalf of the Virginia Company of London and by the grace of His Majesty King James. I am the governor of this colony, Thomas Gates."

Beside him, William elbowed Sam sharply in the ribs. "Did you hear that? The governor's name is Gates, too!"

"I heard." Sam looked at Governor Gates with interest, wondering at the coincidence of his surname. The older man's receding reddish brown hair and matching beard framed a pale, narrow face. In some ways he resembled Sam's father, though his small brown eyes held a much haughtier expression.

Governor Gates next introduced his deputy, Sir Thomas

Dale, who held the official title of Marshall of Virginia, followed by several other important men. Then came a lengthy
lecture about the laws and rules of the colony. Sam's mind
drifted during much of this; there were so many much more
interesting things to focus on, from the other Jamestown
inhabitants, to the rustic expanse of the fort's imposing palisade walls, to the competing scents of vegetation and decay
that wafted on the slight breeze.

Finally the governor stopped speaking, and the new-
comers entered the triangular fort. The interior of the fort
seemed somehow smaller than the outside. It was crammed
with numerous half-timbered buildings that had been
hastily constructed of wattle and daub, most of which made
even the Gates family's modest flat back in London seem
grand by comparison. Dusty dirt paths separated the rows
of barracks and small houses, and the settlement's church
stood in a position of honor set apart from the rest.

Within minutes, Sam and William had secured a room
in one of the barracks inside the fort. Once that was settled,
their minds turned to finding a way to earn a living. A dark-
haired man in his late twenties circulated through the crowd,
loudly offering employment to any newly arrived settler who

was able and willing to work hard.

"What type of employment do you offer?" William asked, stopping the man.

"Ah, you look like a strong lad," the man said with a smile, looking William up and down. "My name is John Rolfe. I intend to export my first crop of tobacco back to England quite soon. I expect to need many more farmhands once people back in London get a taste of my new strain."

"I see," William said eagerly. "I—"

"William," Sam interrupted, grabbing him by the arm and pulling him away. "Begging your pardon, sir, but I must speak with my brother a moment."

"What's the matter?" William demanded, once they were out of earshot. "I was about to secure a job."

Sam shook his head. "Have you not heard of the tobacco grown here in Virginia?" he said. "It has been much talked of back in London as being far inferior to that grown in the Spanish colonies to the south. Nobody yet has been able to make money exporting it from Virginia—if you bond yourself to that Rolfe fellow, you would surely not make the fortune you expect here."

"For once I am grateful that you are so interested in the

dull subjects of reading and current events, little brother!"
William grinned and clapped him on the shoulder. "Many
thanks for the warning. Now, let us find employment where
we can indeed make our fortune!"

In William's case, that didn't take long at all. Within
minutes, he had agreed to go to work assisting the local
blacksmith.

Sam, however, found that most of the farmers and land-
holders cast little more than a dubious glance at his slight
physique and bookish mien before passing him by. Before
long he realized that he would have to convince some of
them that he could work just as hard as the burlier men. But
first he pulled out his notebook again and jotted a few lines
describing the interior of the fort.

"You! Boy! You can read and write?"

Sam looked up from his notebook to find a portly man
with a neat blond beard standing before him. It was clear
from his well-crafted doublet and fine cape and slops that
the man was a gentleman.

"Yes, sir," Sam said. "I was apprenticed to a bookbinder
back in London. I read nearly everything that came through
the shop and helped keep the accounts as well."

"Excellent." The man beamed at him. "You are just the man I am seeking! My name is John Martin. I keep the records here—births, deaths, that sort of thing—and lately I've been attempting to set down the history of this colony as well. Since the departure of Captain Smith, I'm afraid nobody has been chronicling the happenings of Jamestown, and I am finding it quite a task. I could use an assistant."

Sam could not believe his good fortune. Only hours in and already the tide of luck was changing. He quickly agreed to the job and followed his new employer outside the fort through a second entrance at the rear. The trees had been cut back for a good distance beyond the palisades, and the well-worn dirt showed that this path was well traveled.

"You don't live in the fort itself, then?" he asked Mr. Martin.

"Not anymore." Martin glanced over at him. "I had a room in the Quarter for a while after arriving with the First Supply in '08. But when my wife and children came over aboard the *Deliverance* with Lord De La Warr's party, we moved onto our own plot of land."

"You've been here since 1608?" Sam asked curiously. "Then you must have lived through the Starving Time."

"Yes." Martin's face darkened and he looked away. "But I do not speak of that."

"I am sorry to mention it, sir." Sam thought again of the tales he'd heard about the winter of 1609–1610. It was said that by the end of that winter the population of Jamestown had been reduced from around five hundred to less than one hundred. There were terrible tales of desperation, of the eating of horses, dogs, and other domestic animals, even cannibalism. Sam wasn't surprised that Mr. Martin might want to forget it.

But that was more than two years past now. The colony had rebounded, thanks to the timely arrival of Lord De La Warr's ships and subsequent loads of supplies and settlers. Now Sam and his shipmates would add still more to the growing population.

Soon Mr. Martin was leading Sam across a plowed field toward a modest half-timbered house with a thatched roof. A smaller tributary was visible to the northwest, but once out of sight of the James the air was hot and humid. Sam felt himself start to sweat, and he slapped at a mosquito buzzing about his face.

"Why did you not build along the James River?" Sam

asked. "It seems much cooler there."

"It is a fair question, lad." Martin glanced at him. "Sadly, aside from the spot where the fort stands, much of the riverfront is occupied by a great swamp. I shall not speak ill of Captain Smith and Christopher Newport, but they couldn't have chosen a poorer spot than this wretched island for a new settlement." His gaze wandered out toward the wooded land across the tributary. "Then again, numerous villages of the savages surround us on every side. So perhaps there was no better choice after all."

They were nearing the house by now, and suddenly a great commotion rang out from somewhere behind it. The angry squealing of a horse mingled with what sounded like a woman's cries.

"Oh, dear," Martin said with a sigh.

With a gasp, Sam saw a slim, golden-haired girl in her late teens struggling to hang on to the reins of an unruly bay gelding, which dragged her around the corner of the house and then began rearing up repeatedly beside her, several times nearly dropping his forelegs into a large stone water trough nearby.

"Let go!" Sam cried, racing forward. "I'll help you!"

The girl shot him a glance. Before he could reach her, she gave the reins one last tug, bringing the horse's forelegs back to earth and spinning him around in a tight circle.

"Never mind," she called out with a laugh. "Venture and I have reached an understanding, I think."

Sam stopped short as the girl climbed onto the edge of the trough and vaulted onto the gelding's bare back. With a snort, the horse took off at a brisk canter. The girl's laughter drifted behind her as she rode toward the fort.

"Now you have made the acquaintance of my daughter, Elizabeth," Martin told Sam with a wry smile.

Sam didn't answer for a moment. He was still staring after Elizabeth Martin in amazement. It was clear that she was nothing like the girls back in London, who wore their riding habits only to be in fashion and rarely, if ever, actually rode. For a brief moment, Sarah came into his mind, but he shunned the thought immediately. There was no use in dwelling on what could not be.

Just then, a young man rushed out of the house. "Did you see, Father?" he cried. "Liz promised not to mess about with Venture, and there she goes!"

"It's all right, son." Mr. Martin waved a hand toward

Sam. "Did you not hear? A ship has arrived. This is Samuel. He'll be working for me from now on. Samuel, this is my son Harold, known as Hal."

"Pleasure to meet you." Sam stuck out his hand toward Hal, who was stoutly built like his father, with limp blond hair and an immense moon-shaped face with a spot of bright red on each round cheek.

Hal regarded Sam's hand suspiciously, making no move to grasp it with his own. "Does this mean I'll not have to sort all those tiresome papers and maps and drawings anymore?" he asked his father.

Sam withdrew his hand, disliking Hal Martin already. Too bad—it would have been nice to have encountered a friend near his own age in this brand-new place.

Aside from the encounter with Hal, the rest of the afternoon passed pleasantly enough. Sam found Mrs. Martin, the two younger Martin siblings, and the family's maidservant welcoming and kind, and the work he would be doing quite interesting. Elizabeth returned after an hour or two and was properly introduced, and she proved herself just as extraordinary as Sam had first observed, by shaking his hand with a grip as firm as a man's and insisting he call her "Liz" rather than "Miss Elizabeth." The sun was already sinking below the tops of the trees to the west when he finally took his leave of the Martin homestead for the evening and headed off across the fields toward the fort.

I hope William's day at the forge has gone as well as mine, he thought as he picked his way carefully across the uneven ground in the quickly fading light. *Perhaps with a little luck we Gates boys will be able to—*

He let out a gasp and ducked, sensing rather than seeing something whizzing toward his head in the dusk. The rock—for that was what it was—thudded to the ground some distance away, its considerable weight leaving a furrow.

Sam's heart pounded. Putting his fists in the air, he glanced around, wondering if a savage might be lurking just out of sight nearby, watching him. Or perhaps it wasn't a savage after all. . . .

Jasper! he thought.

Since disembarking, he had seen the treasure hunter only from a distance. From what he'd observed, it appeared that Jasper had been among a small group of men hired to dig a second well inside the fort; Sam had made note of this with some relief, hoping it would keep Jasper busy enough to forget all about his dispute with Sam.

But it seemed such hope was in vain. If the rock *had* been thrown by Jasper, then it was clear he hadn't forgotten about Sam or his "treasure map." Sam hurried on and reached the fort without further incident. But his mind was filled with thoughts of Jasper, Elias's letter, and that infernally cryptic engraving on the ship's lantern as he drifted off into his first night's sleep in this strange new land.

Seven

For the next several days, Sam was too busy getting used to life in Jamestown to spare much thought for Jasper or the treasure map. However, he did remember to ask his new boss about Cousin Gilbert.

"Gilbert, Gilbert . . ." Mr. Martin scratched his pale beard thoughtfully. "Aye—I believe I can recall the fellow you mean. Rather short, ears like cabbages?"

"Um, yes?" Sam guessed eagerly, noting the resemblance to Elias in the large ears. "Do you know him?"

"I did," Martin said. "He was lost in the Starving Time. His wife survives him, though. Why do you ask? He was not a relative of yours?"

"No," Sam said, disappointed though not surprised to confirm Gilbert's demise. "His cousin was a friend of mine. Do you know where I might find his widow?"

Martin shrugged. "She is remarried to a Mr. Norton and lives in one of the homes within the fort. Now, about these documents . . ."

Later that day, Sam had enough free time between work and supper to find his way to the Norton house, located at the northern corner of the triangular fort, near the original well.

Mrs. Norton was a plump, agreeable woman with a ruddy face. Her cheerful expression turned sad when Sam mentioned that he'd known Elias. She wiped the soot off her hands on her apron. "I'm sorry to hear he is gone. Gilbert spoke of him and Isaac often. In fact, I have always suspected his last words might have been directed at them."

"Really? What were they?" Sam asked.

She pursed her lips. "I try not to remember much of that time," she said softly. "But I can't forget those words— they seemed to cost him so much to get them out. 'Look to the south,' was what he said. 'Tell them to look to the south.'"

Sam's stomach flip-flopped. That certainly sounded like some sort of clue! "What did he mean by that?" he asked eagerly.

Mrs. Norton shook her head. "I have no idea. Now if you'll excuse me, I must take the pudding off the fire."

Sam was still thinking about his conversation with Gilbert's widow late the next afternoon as he carefully poured fresh ink into one of the wells in Mr. Martin's office. He was so deep in thought that he didn't realize Hal had entered until he spoke.

"Father just told me your surname is Gates," Hal said. "Are you a relation to our governor?"

Noting the respect in his voice, Sam was tempted to say yes. But his honest nature forced him to shake his head. "No, no relation," he said.

"I see." Hal sounded relieved. "I should have guessed. Governor Gates is a great friend of my father's, and also a great hero of Jamestown. I see no family relation there at all." Hal laughed insolently. "Too bad your name doesn't make *you* so brave or successful."

In the past few days, Sam had grown used to Hal's boasting and barbed comments. Hal clearly thought that being the son of a gentleman gave him the right to taunt his father's new worker at will.

"Oh, really?" Sam said, his voice rising. "Don't be so certain I won't find success. For all you know, I might have a sure way of making my fortune here."

"Oh, really?" Hal mimicked Sam's inflection, then laughed again. "Then how come you're here refilling inkwells for my father?"

Sam gritted his teeth, tempted to say more but knowing he shouldn't. It would be foolish to brag about the treasure. Besides, he'd just noticed Liz standing outside the office door listening with an amused smile on her face. As Hal swept out of the room, she entered.

"My brother is a prig, is he not?" Liz asked, her eyes dancing with mischief. "If you wish to push him into the swamp and leave him for the wild beasts to find, I swear not to tell a soul."

Sam laughed. "Thanks. I shall keep that in mind."

Liz perched on the edge of her father's desk, watching as Sam went back to work on the inkwells. "How are you liking life in the colonies thus far?" she asked. "Is it all you were told it would be back in England?"

"Not exactly." Sam chuckled, thinking about the notes he'd been jotting down all week about life in Jamestown. "Life is very different here—much harder." He capped the ink jar and stepped back. "And no chamber pots of pure gold after all," he murmured under his breath.

"What was that?" Liz cocked her head to one side. "Did you say something about lacking chamber pots? Oh dear— I do hope your new home came equipped!"

Sam blushed. "No, er, yes. I mean, that was a line in a play I saw a few years back—*Eastward, Ho!*" he explained quickly. "A character claimed that the riches of the New World meant that all the settlers had chamber pots of gold."

"I see," Liz said. "I believe I recall hearing of that play before I left England. But never mind—I wish to hear more about how you plan to make your fortune." Her tone was light and teasing, but the sparkle in her eyes made Sam not mind the joke at all.

He grinned. "Never mind that," he teased in return. "I wish to know where *you* learned to handle a horse!"

For the next hour, the two of them talked as Sam worked. And the more they talked, the more Sam liked his employer's spirited daughter. When Liz's father came in to dismiss Sam for the day, Liz walked beside him out of the house. For once there was a breeze, making the humid, swamp-scented air more bearable.

"Ah, that's more like it!" Sam tipped his face, still warm

from the stifling heat inside the house, to catch the breeze.

"Just wait until you experience your first Virginia winter," Liz said with a laugh. "You'll miss these hot days then!" She shook her head, still smiling. "As my father is fond of saying, the original settlers could not have chosen a less agreeable spot to live."

Sam chuckled. "Yes, he's already mentioned that to me a time or two. I wonder why no one ever thought to move the settlement elsewhere? Was it fear of the savages?"

Liz shrugged, then glanced at the horizon, where only the last rosy blush of the sun was still faintly visible against the rapidly darkening sky. "Well, good night," she said. "I shall see you tomorrow, Samuel."

"Wait!" Sam impulsively grabbed her hand before she could turn away. "What is the hurry? The evening has just turned pleasant, after all!"

"True. But I must return to help my mother clean up the kitchen."

"Must you?" Sam wheedled playfully, not wanting her to go just yet.

"Indeed. And *you* must be off back to the fort before the wild creatures of the night eat you," Liz said lightly.

"Oh?" Sam returned. "It almost sounds as though you're trying to be rid of me."

"Perhaps I am." A smile played about her lips, but her eyes were anxious as they glanced toward the shadowy forest across the tributary.

Sam wondered if she might not be as brave as she acted. "Shall I walk you back to the house first?"

"No!" she said, even before he'd finished. "It's quite all right. I can make it back on my own."

By now Sam was growing rather suspicious. "Truly, is something going on?" he asked. "Why are you acting so oddly all of a sudden?"

She took a deep breath and an anguished expression darkened her delicate features. For a moment he feared he might have offended her.

"All right," she said abruptly. "I know already from our talks that you are a most agreeable and intelligent person. But can you keep a secret, Samuel Gates?"

"I can," he said immediately, feeling flattered by her compliments.

"I am waiting out here to meet someone."

Sam's heart sank, and the feeling of flattery faded

quickly away. That could mean only one thing—Liz had a male admirer. "I see," he said stiffly. "In that case, I shall leave before he arrives."

"He?" Liz laughed. "No, no it's not a he. It's a she—a girl from the local Powhatan tribe."

"What?" Sam blinked. "Powhatan? You mean the savages?"

"They're not savages!" Liz said quickly with a slight frown. "Matachanna is a person, just like you or me. She knows much of our language already, and she's really quite kind and interesting."

Sam didn't speak for a moment. He was still trying to grasp what Liz had just told him. Naturally he had heard the tales of the young native maiden Matoaka, better known as Pocahontas, who had befriended Captain Smith and learned English. Somehow, though, he hadn't really believed it. Everyone in London said that Smith was rather boastful and prone to embellishment, and so Sam had assumed that the explorer's tales of the savages were exaggerated at best.

Liz was still staring at him, as if daring him to argue. "I trust you'll tell no one of this," she said. "Matachanna is my friend. I won't have you betray her."

"I have no plans to betray anyone," Sam replied. "But I

thought the savages were our enemies? Back in London, they are blamed for most of the losses this colony has suffered over the past few years. And they are said to viciously attack any Englishman who wanders too far from the fort."

Liz shrugged. "Some of that is true, I suppose," she said. "But it has nothing to do with Matachanna. She is not interested in hurting anyone."

Just then there was a rustling in the brush nearby. A girl of around Liz's age peered out—and promptly disappeared again when she spotted Sam.

"Matachanna, wait!" Liz called softly, taking a few steps forward. "It's all right. My friend wants to meet you."

Everything remained still for a moment. Sam held his breath.

Then, finally, the face reappeared. The native girl—Matachanna—stepped clear of her hiding place, allowing Sam a clear look at her.

In some ways, she looked very strange. She was dressed in a knee-length fringed dress made of animal skin, a pair of moccasins, and little else; her long, black hair was partially shaved, revealing earrings dangling from her ears, and the bronze skin of her arms, neck, and shoulders was decorated with multiple tattoos of flowers, snakes, and other things Sam couldn't make out in the dusky light.

"Matachanna, this is Sam," Liz said. "Don't worry, he can be trusted."

"Greetings, Sam." Matachanna's voice was soft, her words accented but clear. "It is good to meet you."

"Thank you." Sam felt awkward. "It is good to meet you, too, Mataho—er, that is, Matchawa—uh . . ."

His voice trailed off as both Liz and Matachanna burst out in peals of laughter. "My name is Matachanna," the girl said, pronouncing each syllable slowly and clearly.

"Matachanna," Sam repeated with a smile, suddenly far more comfortable. "I think I have it now."

"Shall we take a walk?" Liz suggested to Matachanna. "I have thought of many new questions for you."

Matachanna shook her head. "I am sorry, my friend Liz," she said. "I cannot stay here long. My father Wahunsunacock is in my village tonight, and I wish not to be missed." Shooting a cautious glance toward Sam, she added, "He is angry this day with my sister Matoaka, who wished to pay a visit to your village, and his brother Opechancanough is urging him to pull away entirely from any ideas of friendship between our two tribes. I do not wish to give him any reason to attack your people again."

"I understand." Liz sounded disappointed. "Perhaps we can meet again in a few days."

"We shall see." Matachanna sounded a bit doubtful. She was already backing away into the shadows of the thick foliage. "Be careful, my friend." She glanced at Sam. "I hope to see you again, new friend Sam."

With that, she was gone. "Wow," Sam said. "Did she say Matoaka is her sister? Isn't that the other name they call Pocahontas, the native princess written about by Captain Smith?"

"Yes." Liz sounded distracted as she gazed off in the direction in which Matachanna had gone. It was almost fully dark by now, and the opposite side of the river was visible only by the fireflies lighting up the night. "Matachanna and Matoaka are both daughters of the Powhatan werowance."

"Werowance?" Sam repeated.

"That is the name of their leader, their king," Liz explained. "You heard Matachanna say his given name, though I still cannot pronounce it properly." Her worried expression faded as she laughed. "Most settlers refer to him merely as Chief Powhatan, perhaps for that same reason. He rules over all the villages of this region."

They turned and started walking. "Matachanna seems nice," Sam said, kicking away a clump of dirt in their path so that Liz wouldn't stumble. "Not what I was expecting of my first meeting with a savage, I'll admit."

"I know." Liz sighed. "It is too bad things are like this—the fighting, the mistrust. I have heard that it was different back in the earliest days of settlement—like in Roanoke Colony. There, it is said that naturals and settlers lived in harmony and helped one another like brothers."

"Yes," Sam said with a grimace, thinking of all his father had told him of the Lost Colony, including some things that directly contradicted what Liz had said. "And look how *that* turned out. The colony at Roanoke . . ." His voice trailed off as a thought struck him with the force of a thunderbolt.

Liz turned to peer at him in the darkness. "What is it?" she asked with concern. "What's the matter?"

"*Elizabeth!*"

Liz winced as Hal's voice bellowed her name from the direction of the house. "Oh, dear," she said, gathering her skirts. "I must get back before Father sends out a search party. I shall see you tomorrow, Samuel!"

"Good-bye," Sam said, but he was so distracted that for once he barely noticed her departure. He turned and wandered back toward the fort, his brain filled with ideas and a growing sense of excitement. He wasn't certain . . . but he thought he might have just figured out Gilbert's latest clue!

Eight

The next morning, Sam did some quick research in Mr. Martin's records. Then he made an excuse to go back inside the fort.

He was hurrying along the hard-packed dirt path between the settlement's church and main storehouse when he heard someone calling his name. Stopping short and turning, he was startled to see Governor Gates striding toward him.

"My boy!" the governor said, beaming as he reached Sam. "I have been hoping to see you—I just encountered your delightful brother, William, at the forge. I simply had to meet the young men who share my surname!"

Sam was distracted by thoughts of his errand, but he forced a smile. He'd heard that Governor Gates was very strict and tolerated no misconduct within the colony. It wouldn't do to insult him.

"Indeed," he said as the governor shook his hand. "William and I were honored to discover the coincidence when we first arrived here in Jamestown."

The governor chuckled. "As well you should be." He winked broadly. "I trust I won't hear tales of you two pretending to be my sons or nephews to curry favor, shall I?"

"Certainly not!" Sam laughed along, even though the joke didn't seem particularly funny.

The governor squinted at the sun overhead. "I'd best be off—I would not like to be late for today's meeting with Sir Dale and Mr. Morehead," he said self-importantly. "It was a pleasure to make your acquaintance, young Mr. Gates."

"The honor is entirely mine," Sam replied. He was tempted to add "old Mr. Gates," but figured the governor might not see the humor.

The governor moved on, leaving Sam free to continue his quest. He quickly found his destination—the shoemaker's workshop near the center of town. When he entered, a gray-bearded man of around fifty looked up from his last, where he was working a piece of tanned leather with an awl, and wiped the sweat from his eyes with the back of one hand.

"Help you, son?" he asked with a friendly nod.

Sam introduced himself. "Are you John Billings?" he asked. "I heard you sailed with John White back in 1590 when he discovered the missing colonists at Roanoke."

The man burst into hearty laughter. "I am indeed John Billings," he said, standing up and reaching for a rag to wipe off his hands. "But I'm afraid you are mistaken about the rest. I only arrived here in the New World recently—I came with the governor and his three hundred settlers just two years since, and that was the first time I'd set foot outside of England."

"Oh." Sam's shoulders slumped. He'd been excited at the idea that he might be able to confirm his theory with a first-hand source.

"No, it was my late Uncle Stephen that sailed with White about twenty years ago, now," Billings said amiably, stepping across his shop to grab another piece of leather. "P'raps that's how you got mixed up. See, I've been known to tell a tale or two of adventure down at the tavern, even if the adventures aren't always my own." He guffawed at his own comment.

"Really?" Sam's heart beat faster again. "I'd love to hear what you know about your uncle's adventures."

"All right, my boy. Uncle Stephen talked about it so often once he returned to London that I know the stories by heart." Billings went back to work as he spoke, shaping what would become a new leather shoe. "He talked of how Governor White was very eager to return to see his granddaughter, Virginia Dare. Did you know she was the first English citizen born in the New World?"

Sam nodded. "So what happened when they got there?"

"White hadn't seen the child or its mother, his daughter Eleanor, in some two and a half years, thanks to the trouble with the infernal Spanish that delayed his return to the colony." Billings scowled, then turned to spit on the floor. But his genial expression returned almost immediately. "My uncle claimed that they reached land on young Virginia's third birthday, though I know not if that was true—my uncle was prone to tall tales at times." He winked at Sam. "In any case, they landed and found no settlers, and no sign of what might have become of them, aside from a single word carved on a post— 'Croatoan.'"

"What does that mean?" Sam asked. "Did your uncle say?"

Billings glanced up from his work and shrugged. "Evidently, White believed it meant the settlers hadn't been removed by force," he said. "They'd previously arranged with him to carve a Maltese cross onto a tree if they were attacked or in danger. So he thought the Croatoan mark meant they'd gone to a nearby island to live with the native tribe by that name."

"And had they?"

"Nobody knows." Billings flipped over his piece of leather and reached for a needle. "White wasn't able to check, as a storm was coming, and the men with him refused to stay any longer. So the whole thing remains a mystery more than twenty years later."

Sam smiled. "Thank you," he said. "That's a very interesting story indeed."

"I know some better ones, if you've a mind for such things," Billings said. "Perhaps you'd like to hear about the wreck of Governor Gates's ship, the *Sea Venture*, on the island of Bermuda, and all the hardships we experienced on that exotic isle during which we built two new ships from scratch and then finally managed to make it here to Jamestown some nine months later."

"I'd love to," Sam said, already backing toward the door. "But perhaps another time—I must return to work now."

He rushed off, eager to find Liz and ask if she knew

anything of the Croatoan tribe, or perhaps could find out from Matachanna. *From what she said, it seems that all the native people in a wide radius are related to one another under the leadership of this Chief Powhatan,* he thought as he hurried past several buildings, including the blacksmith's forge where his brother worked. *Perhaps Matachanna will be able to help me track down these Croatoans, and . . .*

He stopped short at the sound of a familiar female laugh. It was coming from within the forge. Barely noticing the waves of intense heat emanating from inside, he stepped closer and peered in through the door. Sure enough, Liz was there, smiling and laughing and fanning herself with one hand as she chatted with Sam's brother.

William was shirtless and his muscular torso glowed red with heat and sweat. He was leaning on a large hammer and grinning down at Liz with the same expression he'd often turned upon the most beautiful young ladies back in London.

Sam's stomach clenched at the sight of them standing so close together. But he shook off the feeling and called out a greeting.

"Little brother!" William called back, raising a hand to

him. "Have you met the lovely Elizabeth Martin yet?"

"Many times," Sam replied. A scruffy-looking black-and-white dog that had been napping beneath a table leaped up in a flurry of barking, though Sam was able to fend it off easily with one foot. "I work for her father, remember?"

"Oh, indeed!" William let out a laugh. He leaned over and, with one easy motion, tossed a sizable log onto the flames of the forge before hauling the leaping dog back out of the way. "I must be addle-brained in the presence of such beauty."

Liz smiled. "Or perhaps it's the heat," she responded. "In any case, William, thanks for taking my father's order. He may stop by to discuss it with you later—he's here in the fort for a meeting this morning." Then she turned her smile on Sam. "Did Father send you to find me? I admit I've been gone longer than I intended."

"No," Sam replied. "I just happened to be passing and heard you. Shall we walk together back to your father's house?"

"Better watch out for that one, Elizabeth," William called out with a laugh as they left the forge. "He may look innocent, but with his clever mind and quick wit, he was the terror of every pretty young lady in London!"

Sam blushed, wishing he could beat William over the head with his own hammer for such a comment. "Sorry about that," he said to Liz. "William thinks he's amusing."

"Yes." Liz glanced over her shoulder at the forge as they turned down the path leading to the fort's nearest exit. "He's very strong, your brother, isn't he?"

Desperate to avoid further talk of William and recapture the nice, intimate feeling the two of them had shared the evening before, he blurted out, "Can you keep a secret?"

Liz shot him a surprised look. "Of course. What is it?"

Before he could think twice about the wisdom of confiding in her, he told Liz about Elias and his clue to a treasure. ". . . and unfortunately, he died during the journey, but with his last breath he left it to me to continue his quest," he finished, purposely leaving out any mention of Jasper.

Liz looked skeptical. "A treasure? Here?" she said. "Don't be too sure. Everyone knows the so-called gold the first settlers sent back was a worthless look-alike—pyrite, I think they called it. And the minerals they sent to England amounted to nothing, either."

"This is different," Sam insisted. "See, Elias's cousin sent a letter. . . ."

As they walked, he filled her in on the letter and its clues and how they had led him in turn to the engraving on the ship's lantern. Before long her skeptical expression turned to one of fascination.

"And what has all of this to do with Roanoke?" she prompted, after Sam had described his recent conversation with the shoemaker. "Why did you wish to speak with Mr. Billings?"

"Well, it was thanks to you that I made the connection," Sam said. "Remember how you mentioned the lost Roanoke colony yesterday? That reminded me that the verse on the lantern was attributed 'White, 1590.' I realized it must refer to Governor John White, who discovered in that year that the colony had been lost."

Liz's eyes lit up. "I see!" she cried. "Your friend Elias's cousin must have seen that lantern on the *Constant*."

"Right." Sam stopped short and smiled at her. They had reached a quiet area just a few yards inside the exit from the fort. "And then based a clue on the verse, planting a coded message to his cousins in his letter so they would be sure to take that particular ship over and figure out the meaning once they saw the verse."

"Er—and that meaning is what, exactly?" Liz asked.

"Think about it," Sam urged. "The verse says '*Those lost leave their mark.*' Their mark—that would be the mark on the tree, the word Croatoan, which was left by the lost colonists. The treasure must be hidden in Roanoke, near that tree!" He grinned, pleased with his own deduction. "That's one of the things I wished to ask you. How far is Roanoke from here?"

Liz shook her head. "Far," she said plainly. "Very far. It would take days."

"Oh." Sam's heart dropped like a stone. He had only the vaguest idea of the geography of the New World and had expected Roanoke Colony might be a few hours' journey. But no—a journey of many days was impossibly far.

How am I going to get there? he thought with a rush of despair, clutching the ring he still wore around his neck. *It will be a long time before I can ever expect to afford a horse. . . .*

"Are you certain the treasure is in Roanoke, though?" Liz asked thoughtfully. "It seems odd that it would be hidden so far from Jamestown. How would Gilbert have managed to carry it so far?"

"I don't know." Sam's mind was still so full of his own thoughts that he barely registered her words. "Perhaps he never moved it in the first place. If the treasure Gilbert mentioned is the riches of the Lost Colony, left for him by his uncle, where else would it be?"

"Are you certain that's the treasure Gilbert meant?" Liz asked. "Unless there's something you haven't told me, it doesn't sound as if he was that specific."

"True," Sam admitted, taking more notice of what she was saying. "But Gilbert's uncle was at Roanoke. What other treasure would it be?"

"There are plenty of tales of treasure flying about," Liz pointed out. "It could be something else entirely. In which case, what if the Croatoan mark isn't the location of the treasure itself, but rather another clue to the true location?"

Sam blinked, realizing that in the excitement of figuring out the lantern clue and the subsequent disappointment of discovering that Roanoke was so far away, he hadn't thought of that possibility. "Perhaps you're right," he said slowly. "But if so, what could it possibly mean?"

The two of them stood in silence for a moment,

thinking about his question. But they were interrupted by Hal's disagreeable voice.

"Oi! Office boy!" Hal called, hurrying toward them through the fort's entrance. "What are you doing here? You're meant to be sorting papers or some such."

Liz frowned at her brother. "What are *you* doing here?" she asked him. "Last I heard, Father told you to cut fence rails today."

Hal made a face. "Hold your tongue, sister. Remember, men do not like ladies to be too saucy or too bossy."

"A-ha! Why, here's my young namesake again!" The governor's booming voice interrupted before Liz could respond. He was walking toward them with several other important-looking gentlemen, including Mr. Martin. "And look, Martin. Isn't that your boy? He must have sensed you volunteered him for duty." He chuckled, and the other men followed his lead.

"Huh?" Hal looked confused as he glanced at his father.

But it was one of the other men who spoke next, a well-known gentleman of the colony by the name of Francis Q. Morehead. "We need some work done for the good of the settlement," Morehead said in an officious voice. He turned away from Hal to look Sam up and down with close-set gray eyes beneath shaggy black brows. "You two young men look just right for the task."

The men went on to explain that they were looking for a couple of volunteers to widen a path through the woods on the far side of the tributary. It led to a smaller island where some cattle and sheep owned by Morehead and the governor had been set loose to graze. Sam suspected the two men were looking for someone to take on a task they wished not to be bothered with themselves, and that Mr. Martin was currying favor by volunteering his son and employee to take care of it. From the expression on Liz's face, he guessed she was entertaining similar thoughts. But both kept such ideas to themselves.

"Of course," Sam said. "We can get started right now and be finished before dinner. Right, Hal?"

Hal looked truculent. "But, Father," he whined. "You know the heat disagrees with me, and—"

"My son is happy to help." Martin said loudly, cutting him off. "Get on with you now, Hal."

"When you've reached the island, be certain to ford the stream and check on the animals," Morehead added. "We require a count so as to know if the savages have stolen any."

"Of course," Sam said politely, though at the mention of "savages" he couldn't help but think of the gentle and intelligent Matachanna.

The governor stepped forward and clapped Sam on the back. "There we go," he said jovially. "Always ready to help. Just like a Gates, eh?" He winked at Sam before turning away with the other men.

Hal made a face at Sam behind their backs. "'Just like a Gates, eh?'" he mimicked with great bad temper.

Sam and Hal walked Liz home, picked up tools there, and then made their way across the river to the path in question. It was clear that no one had tended to it in quite a while; vines twined across it, and small saplings blocked the way every few feet.

"This should be great fun," Sam muttered. He stepped forward and swung his ax at the first sapling.

Hal halfheartedly yanked at a vine. "We should have brought a billhook to help clear this brush," he announced. "Keep at it—I shall run home and fetch one." Before Sam could protest, he was gone.

Sam grimaced. He might have expected Hal to duck out

of the work at his earliest opportunity. He could only hope he would return at some point, whether on his own or chased back by Liz or one of their parents.

In the meantime, he continued on his own. Clearing the trail was tough, dirty work. But it did allow him plenty of time to think about his treasure quest.

He was deep in thought but had reached no new conclusions by the time he reached the creek separating him from the island where the livestock were grazing. He sat down on the rocky shore and mopped the sweat from his brow. The water was only a few yards across, but deep and fast-moving as it tumbled down a steep slope toward the James River in the unseen distance. Sam could see several sheep and a heifer from where he was sitting, and for a moment he was tempted to leave it at that.

Then he remembered that Mr. Morehead was expecting a head count. With a groan, he climbed to his feet and glanced around, hoping that Hal might return in time to handle this part at least. But there was no sign of life anywhere on his side of the creek, aside from a few small birds flitting about.

"Typical," he muttered, with a flash of irritation.

Removing his shoes, he started across the creek. The thigh-high cold water felt good after his exertion, but he stayed focused, moving carefully. The streambed was uneven and rocky, and he knew that one slip or bad step could send him tumbling head over heels downstream with the rushing current.

About halfway across, he glanced at the far side to gauge his progress. One of the sheep was grazing on a few sparse tufts near the water. Just then it suddenly raised its head, staring off across the stream.

Hoping the sheep hadn't spotted a bear or some other fearsome predator, Sam glanced back over his shoulder. He gasped at what he saw, which was much more frightening than a bear.

"Jasper!" he blurted out.

The lanky treasure hunter was standing on the shore with a bow and arrow in his hand. For one dizzying moment Sam thought the older man meant to poach the sheep.

But Jasper wasn't looking at the sheep. With an evil smile, he cocked an arrow and pointed it directly at Sam. Before Sam could react, the arrow was flying toward him, and a second later he felt a terrible fiery pain radiate out from his left shoulder.

"Aaah!" he cried, struggling to maintain his precarious footing.

But it was no use. The arrow's blow had thrown him off balance. He felt himself falling forward, straight toward a jagged patch of rocks protruding from the rushing water.

Sam tried to put his hand out to break the fall, but the motion only wrenched his injured shoulder hard enough to make him scream. A second later, his head struck the rocks with a sickening thud.

As he lost consciousness, he felt the cold water close over his face.

Nine

Sam returned to consciousness with a cough. As he choked up a lungful of water, he remembered what had happened, and his eyes flew open. He found himself looking up into a concerned moon-shaped face.

"Hal?" he wheezed, then coughed again.

"Thank the Lord!" Hal exclaimed, rocking back on his heels. "I thought you were a goner."

Sam became painfully aware of a throbbing in his shoulder. Rolling his eyes over that way, he saw a bloody gash that made his stomach churn. At least it appeared that the cold stream water had limited the bleeding somewhat.

Hal was looking at the wound, too, his nose wrinkled with distaste. "What was it that attacked you?" he asked. "A bear?"

"What? No!" Sam struggled to sit up, wincing at the pain. He gingerly poked at the wound, pushing aside torn bits of fabric from his clothing. "It was Jasper—he shot me with an arrow!"

He was badly shaken by what had happened. For a while it had seemed possible to forget his trouble with Jasper on the ship. After all, he'd barely seen the man since arriving in Jamestown. But it seemed that Jasper hadn't forgotten anything. He'd merely been biding his time, waiting for an opportunity to take Sam out so he could get his hands on what he thought was a treasure map. This most recent attack could only mean that Jasper was as convinced as ever that Sam was on to something of great value.

"What? Someone shot you with an arrow?" Hal looked skeptical. "Are you seeing savages or something. Come, now—how hard did you hit your head?"

"But didn't you see him?" Sam looked around wildly, half expecting Jasper to step out from behind a tree with that nasty grin and another arrow to finish the job. "How did you get me out of the water, anyway?"

"What do you think? I dragged you," Hal retorted. "And for such a skinny fellow, you weigh as much as an ox!" He shrugged. "Lucky for you I'm no coward. I think I heard the bear or whatever it was crashing off through the woods when I arrived." He puffed out his chest. "But I ignored it and waded straight out to peel you off that tree where you were stuck. Good thing your head was above water, for it took an age to work you loose again."

Sam glanced downstream and spotted a fallen tree trunk a few yards away. After he'd passed out, he must have washed down and been caught up against the tree.

Now that his head was starting to clear, Sam realized that it might be better if Hal didn't believe him. Better for Hal to think it was a bear than that he become overly curious about exactly who Jasper was and why he might be out to get Sam.

"Perhaps it *was* a wild animal after all." Sam put a hand to his head, feigning confusion. "I don't remember much."

Hal shrugged, already seeming to have lost interest. "Did you get the livestock counted yet?"

Hal's moment of niceness over, they completed the task, picking their way carefully across to the island. In his usual lazy fashion, Hal managed to make Sam do most of the work of counting the animals, even though Sam's head and shoulder were both aching mightily.

Finally they finished and headed for home. By this time, Sam was well worn out. His head hurt, the pain in his shoulder had spread down through his arm and half his torso, and all he wanted to do was fall in a heap upon the ground and pass out for a long while. It was all he could do to put one foot in front of the other as he followed Hal down the freshly cleared trail.

They were about halfway home by Sam's hazy reckoning when Hal suddenly spun around, pale-faced and frightened-looking. He grabbed Sam by the arm—his uninjured one, fortunately—and yanked him behind a nearby thicket of shrubs and vines.

"Hush!" he hissed urgently when Sam opened his mouth to ask what he was doing.

A second later Sam heard voices. He tilted his head to one side, trying to make out what they were saying, but it sounded like gibberish. For a moment he feared that blow to the head had addled his brains more than he'd realized.

But then several figures came into view, and his eyes widened with understanding. It was a group of natives!

Aside from Matachanna, Sam had yet to see a native up close, and he watched the approaching men with interest. The tallest of the group was also the oldest, with a weather-beaten, dignified face and a large copper pendant resting on his bare chest. Beside him walked another man near the same age, though a bit shorter and thicker in build, and wearing a fiercer expression on his face. The others in the group walked a little behind those two, carrying what appeared to be the spoils of a successful hunting party.

When the natives had passed safely out of sight and hearing again, Hal turned to Sam with wide eyes. "Did you see that?" he whispered, glancing around nervously as if more savages might be waiting to pop out of the brush behind him. "I'm not certain, but I think that tall one is the savage they call Chief Powhatan! The other one might be his brother. He has a long, ridiculous name like they all do. The brother is said to be more warlike and vicious than even the rest of the savages. It's said he convinces the chief to mistrust our people!"

"Really?" Sam gazed toward where the men had passed with even greater interest. Seeing Chief Powhatan felt a bit like the time that his mother had taken him out as a small child to see Elizabeth the Virgin Queen pass by in a parade. "That was really Chief Powhatan? I wish we could have stepped out and met him."

"Are you loony?" Hal stared at him with true shock. "Meet the king of the savages? *Any* savage would as soon cut our throats as look at us!"

Sam almost opened his mouth to protest that he'd met at least one "savage" who wasn't that way. But he quickly thought better of it. He'd promised to keep Liz's secret, and he meant to honor his word.

When they reached the Martin home, they found Liz outside tending to the herb garden near the house. She immediately dropped her hoe when she spotted Sam.

"Sam! What happened to you?" she cried with concern. "You're all wet—and is that blood?"

Hal smirked. "He lost a fight with a bear," he said. "Good thing I came along when I did, or the savages would've found him and had him for dinner."

"Come inside." Ignoring her brother's pompous remark, Liz tugged on Sam's good arm. "Let's get you fixed up."

Even though it hurt every time Liz touched his wound or moved his arm, Sam found himself enjoying the attention. It was nice to be fussed over by her. She cleaned the wound in the kitchen, then brought him into her father's office where the light was better so she could bandage it with a scrap of linen.

"There," she said, tying off the bandage. "Mustn't have

been a very fierce bear—there's only one mark, though it is rather deep."

"It wasn't a bear." Sam glanced around. Hal had wandered off soon after they'd arrived home, Mrs. Martin and the housegirl were busy in the kitchen, and there was no sign of Mr. Martin. "It was an arrow."

Her eyes widened with shock as he filled her in on what had happened. "Why didn't you tell me before about this Jasper?" she exclaimed. "He sounds like a bad sort indeed!"

"I know." Sam shook his head. "And it seems he'll stop at nothing to get that letter."

"I trust you have it well hidden?"

Sam shrugged. "Not so very well," he admitted. "It is beneath my bed pillow. But I shall find a better place tonight."

"Good." Liz reached over to adjust his bandage. "You shall need to be careful until you unearth the treasure."

"I know." Sam stood and stretched his arm carefully, testing how far he could move it without disturbing his bandage or causing more pain. "My shoulder will help me remember that for a good while, I suspect. Oh! I nearly forgot—on the way home, Hal and I encountered some native men, and Hal claims that one of them was Chief Powhatan!"

"Really?" Liz looked surprised. "Did he see you?"

"No. Hal dragged me into hiding until they'd passed."

"It is probably just as well," Liz said. "Matachanna tells me that her father isn't pleased with any of us settlers at the moment. It was bad enough when Captain Smith was here—evidently he had his ways of convincing the natives to cooperate. But Father says that things have been much worse between the two peoples since Smith left. That is why Matachanna must sneak about in order to meet with me."

"Hal also said the chief's brother was among the party. He didn't know his name."

"It is something like—er—Opechancanough, I think?" Liz said. "Matachanna mentioned him the last time we met. No—not the last time, that was when you met her. The time before that."

"Oh, really? And exactly how many times have you met in secret with Chief Powhatan's daughter, sister?" Hal stepped into view in the doorway.

"Have you been lurking out of sight listening to us?" Liz cried. "You rat!"

"Perhaps I am a rat," Hal said with a smirk. "But at least I do not consort with savages. I wonder what Father would say if he knew about this?"

"You wouldn't dare!" Liz clenched her fists at her sides, her pretty face going red. "Swear you will not tell him, Hal. Swear it!"

"On one condition." Hal turned to include Sam in his smug gaze. "Tell me more of this treasure you mentioned."

Sam's jaw dropped, and he shared a dismayed glance with Liz. She shook her head, her mouth little more than a grim line.

"We shall tell you nothing," she told Hal, tilting her chin up defiantly. "I care not if Father scolds me."

"Oh, really?" Hal glanced at Sam. "I heard him say he met this savage girl as well. I'm sure Father might have something to say about his employee engaging in such activity. Do you care about *that*, sister?"

"You absolute *rat*!" Liz cried, leaping toward Hal with both fists raised.

He grabbed her arms and swung her away. "Hey!" he exclaimed. "Quit that!"

"Stop!" Sam cried. "It's all right, Liz. We should just go

ahead and tell him everything."

"But—" Liz began.

"It doesn't matter," Sam interrupted, knowing that there was no point in arguing. Hal had them, and he was just clever enough to know it. Taking a deep breath, he turned to face the other young man. "It all started with this fellow I met on the ship over . . ."

He continued on, telling Hal the whole story. By the time he finished, he even felt better about doing so. Hadn't sharing it with Liz helped him already? Perhaps Hal, too, would have ideas of his own to add. He might be insufferable, but he wasn't entirely stupid.

"I see," Hal said when he'd heard it all. "So have you worked out where the treasure is buried?"

"Not yet," Sam said. "We're trying to puzzle out what that Croatoan clue might mean, if indeed Liz is correct and it's not a direct indication of the treasure's location."

Hal was silent for a moment, stroking his plump chin. "Well, what about this Jasper chap?" he said. "Perhaps you should stop fighting and work with him as he suggested to you on the ship that time."

"What?" Sam shook his head firmly. "Absolutely not."

"But why not?" Hal demanded. "I think I've seen this Jasper around the settlement. He's older than us and surely knows more. I even saw him drinking ale at the tavern with Francis Q. Morehead. Now, I wouldn't expect one such as you to realize it, but Mr. Morehead is one of the wealthiest men in the colonies and very well connected in the Virginia Company." He shrugged. "In any case, we have the map, right? Surely Jasper is reasonable enough to realize that means we should get the larger share of the treasure."

"Did you say 'we?'" Liz said. "Since when are you a part of this?"

Hal ignored her. "I say we approach Jasper and see if we can cut a deal."

"I said no!" Sam said again. "Besides, Jasper doesn't even know it's a letter—he seems to believe it's a treasure map. I'd prefer to keep him in the dark."

Hal's round face was taking on a mulish expression. "Well, I think you're being foolish," he said. "Jasper could help us."

"I don't care," Sam retorted. "It is my quest and my decision."

They continued arguing until they were interrupted by

Mr. Martin returning home. He bustled into the office, wanting to hear how the livestock counting had gone. After that, Hal hurried off and Sam saw no more of him for the rest of the day.

That evening Sam rushed through his meal of cold left-overs and then went straight to bed. His head still ached from the day's adventures, and his shoulder was throbbing. The idea of sinking into sleep was as blissful an idea as he'd ever had.

But as he pulled the bedclothes over himself, he stuck his hand under the pillow, remembering Liz's admonition about finding a better hiding place for Gilbert's letter. He sat bolt upright as his hand found nothing.

The letter was gone!

Ten

"Hal!" Sam muttered furiously. Immediately forgetting his exhaustion and aching head, he leaped out of bed and threw his clothes back on.

No wonder he hadn't seen Hal much that afternoon! Sam had assumed that Hal had sneaked off to hide from work, as usual. Instead it seemed he'd snuck off to steal the letter. He must have overheard Sam telling Liz where it was hidden and had realized there was no time to lose.

Luckily, Sam had a pretty good idea where he might find Hal and the map. Tiptoeing out past William, who was mending a pair of breeches by the firelight, he hurried toward the barracks on the opposite end of the fort where he knew Jasper had a room.

It was nearly full dark, but the moon and the sentries' torches at the bulwarks gave Sam enough light to see his way to the other barracks. It also offered enough light to see Hal himself standing in the street just outside. Jasper was nowhere in sight. Instead, Hal was facing two men on horseback.

The sound of Hal's insufferable whine drifted to Sam on the breeze when he was still at least twenty paces away. "My apologies, sir," Hal was saying with a touch of panic in his voice. "Really, I meant no harm! I swear it!"

"Swear all you like!" one of the men snarled. "I nearly came off when you darted out and spooked our horses!"

"I did not mean to do it, sir. I swear it! I swear it!" Hal insisted.

As Sam came closer, he could see that the two horses were indeed a bit up-headed and snorty, though their riders had them well in hand. The second rider urged his mount a step or two closer to Hal.

"I know your father would not approve of such behavior, boy," he said, the stern, booming voice revealing him to be Governor Gates. "He is aware that we are a society of rules. He might thank us to teach you a lesson, eh, Francis?"

The first man, whom Sam now recognized as Francis Q. Morehead, barked out a merciless laugh. "Indeed. Shall I have the first lash, or would you like the honor, Governor?"

"Please, sir! No!" Hal squealed, crouching back against the building.

Just then Sam's foot kicked a loose stone. At the sound

of it skittering across the ground, the two men turned and peered at him, squinting against the dark.

"Who goes there?" the governor demanded.

"It is I, Samuel Gates, sir." Sam stepped forward. "Good evening to you. And to you, sir," he added with a bow in Morehead's direction.

Morehead merely nodded curtly, but the governor was smiling now. "I say," Gates said, sounding much friendlier than he had a moment earlier. "Morehead, have you made the acquaintance of my young namesake? He came with the last load of settlers."

"Hmm," Morehead said, seeming disinterested as he continued to glare at Hal.

"That's right!" Hal called out. "Sam is a great friend of mine, Governor! He works for my father, remember? We cleared the way to your livestock together earlier?"

Great friends, eh? Sam thought with a glance at Hal. *That must have happened when I wasn't paying attention.*

"Ah, perhaps this changes things," the governor said. "It had slipped my mind that this fellow was a friend of yours, young Gates. He is, is he not?"

Sam was tempted to say no. He hadn't forgotten the

errand that had brought him there—the stolen letter. He was certain it was somewhere on Hal's person at that very moment, if he hadn't given it to Jasper already.

"Sam?" Hal whined. "Tell him! We are friends, are we not? Why, we spent hours together today clearing that trail through the woods!"

That didn't make Sam feel any friendlier toward him. After all, hadn't Hal abandoned him to do all the work, which had also allowed Jasper to catch him alone?

Still, his sense of decency wouldn't let him deny Hal in his time of need. "Yes," he said to the governor. "Hal is a great friend of mine. In fact, he saved my life earlier this day when I'd been injured and fallen unconscious in the stream."

"Indeed?" The governor looked impressed as he shot Hal a glance. "Very well, then. Let's move on, Francis, and leave these two young men alone. No harm done, after all."

Morehead looked ready to protest, but finally assented. "See to it that I do not lay eyes upon you anytime soon, my boy," he said to Hal as he turned his horse away.

"Of course, sir. Very well, sir." Hal smiled and nodded.

As soon as the two older men had ridden off, he collapsed against the wall. "Whew!" he exclaimed, mopping his broad brow. "Good thing you happened by, Gates. That Morehead is as mean as a snake! And the governor's not much better." He shot a nervous glance after the men, as if fearing they might hear his words. "Anyway, I suppose now we can say we're even. I saved you this morning, and then you saved me."

Sam didn't return Hal's smile. He held out his hand.

"My letter, please," he said sternly.

Hal's smile faded. "What are you talking about?"

"You know. Now give it back."

By now Hal was scowling. "Or what?" he demanded. "You'll tell your best friend the governor all sorts of lies about me? You'll have him call Mr. Morehead to give me a beating?"

Sam didn't bother to answer. His hand stayed out-stretched, unwavering.

"Fine!" Hal's full lips pursed into a pout as he yanked a rolled-up piece of paper out of his doublet. "No need to blackmail me. I can see how this is going to be; I'll save you the negotiations."

Sam took the paper, glanced at it to make sure it was Gilbert's letter, then tucked it away in his own clothes.

"Thank you," he said. "But I wasn't planning to blackmail you."

Hal rolled his eyes. "No?" he said, clearly disbelieving.

"No. My parents did not rear me to do such things," Sam said. "Besides, I am no good at such negotiations."

Hal frowned. "That's a fine trick—making me sweat like that." Then he shrugged, his expression lightening. "Oh, well. We're still a team, right?"

"As much as we ever were," Sam replied.

Hal looked suspicious. "Very well," he said. "Just remember, if you try anything sneaky, like cutting me out of my share of the treasure, I'll be very angry. So angry I might have to tell my father about Elizabeth's little pet savage. If he ever heard she was sneaking off to consort with those creatures, she might as well run off and live with them as those crazy colonists from Roanoke are said to have done." He shrugged. "Because she'd be better off taking her chances with the king of the savages than facing my father when he's angry."

Sam gasped, suddenly forgiving Hal all his bad temper and silly threats. "That's it!" he cried.

Eleven

"That's what?" Hal asked with a frown, peering at Sam in the dim glow from the closest lantern. "What are you on about now?"

Sam shook his head. "We need to get your sister," he said, his heart beating faster with the idea jumping around in his head. "I have an idea."

"About the treasure?" Hal suddenly looked much more interested. "What is it, then? Tell me!"

"I will—when we get Liz." Sam turned and hurried toward the back exit of the fort. Despite Hal's continuing entreaties, he refused to say another word until they reached the Martin home.

Fortunately Liz was still up, banking the fire for the night. Soon all three of them were huddled before the fireplace.

"What is it?" Liz looked from one of the young men to the other. "What are you both doing out so late?"

"Never mind that," Sam said. Now that they were all together, he was eager to have his idea heard. "I just realized something. We've been focusing only on the first line of that verse from the ship— *'Those lost leave their mark.'* But what about the second line? It might be just as important."

"What was it again?" Liz asked, already looking intrigued. "Something about the crown, right?"

"*'Hail the crown, heed the dark,'*" Sam quoted. "Couldn't that be part of the clue?"

Hal looked skeptical. "Sounds like gibberish to me," he said. "What's it mean, anyway?"

"Does it have something to do with King James?" Liz asked uncertainly. "If we're supposed to look at his crown or some such . . ."

Sam shook his head. "Gilbert wouldn't make something like that a clue," he said. "But perhaps he meant us to look to a more local leader. Someone like the governor, perhaps?"

"But he doesn't wear any kind of crown," Hal said.

"No," Liz said. "But there's another local 'king' who often does—Chief Powhatan! Could it mean him?"

"Perhaps," Sam said. "But we can't forget the first part, remember—that was clearly pointing us toward Roanoke Colony."

"Clearly," Hal put in, with more than a touch of his usual sarcasm.

Sam ignored the comment, staring at Liz with growing excitement. "But you did say there was a Croatoan tribe, correct? I think the clue means to point us toward that tribe's leader."

"I .see!" Liz exclaimed, looking just as excited as Sam felt. "Perhaps there's a clue hidden in the Croatoan werowance's ceremonial headdress or something like that— that would be close to a 'crown,' wouldn't it?"

"Or the word could refer to the crown of his head," Hal said, finally starting to catch some of the others' excitement. "Most of the savages have dark hair—heed the dark, right?"

Sam smiled at him. "Good thinking," he said. "Either of those ideas could be correct. The best way to know for sure is to . . ." His voice trailed off as he realized the truth.

"Get a look at that Croatoan chief," Liz finished with a frown. "Oh. How are we supposed to do that?"

Sam realized they were right back where they'd started. If they couldn't manage the journey to the remains of Roanoke Colony to check that mark on the post, they would be even less likely able to travel to the Croatoans' home island somewhere in the same vicinity and track down a werowance who might or might not still be there all these years later.

Sam's shoulders slumped. Trying to solve Gilbert's coded clues was much like jumping one's horse over furrows in a field—a series of leaps that felt like flying, followed each time by a rather painful thud back to earth.

"Never mind," Liz said with a sigh. "I'll discuss all this with Matachanna next chance I get. From what she has mentioned in the past, most of the tribes from here to Florida are interconnected in one way or another. Perhaps she can help figure out a way to get us the information we need without a journey to Roanoke."

With that, the three of them parted ways for the night, each one lost in thoughts of unfindable treasure.

The next morning, Sam spotted Liz perched on the edge of one of the big stone water troughs in front of her house. He was still feeling dejected since hitting the latest block in the quest, and his slow steps reflected that mindset. But his pace picked up slightly when he spotted her. She was obviously waiting for him; as soon as she noticed him coming, she jumped to her feet and hurried to meet him, holding her skirts up and away from the heavy morning dew.

"At last!" she cried, her eyes sparkling. "I thought you'd never arrive. I have news from Matachanna!"

"Already?" Sam was surprised.

She nodded. "I saw her this morning while dumping out the chamber pots by the river," she said, squinting against the morning sun. "I told her of our latest theory, and you shall never believe what she told me in return!"

"What is it?" Sam asked, not really expecting much but still affected enough by her obvious joy to smile.

"She says that there is a Croatoan headdress that is well-known among all the tribes of the coastland," she said. "It once belonged to Wingina, the native chief who was killed by a man named Lane from the Roanoke colony."

Sam nodded. He had read of Ralph Lane and his many troubles with the natives. But he still didn't see how this was good news. Even if they had now confirmed that such a headdress existed, it didn't help them figure out how to get a look at it.

But Liz wasn't finished. "Matachanna also says that Wingina's headdress was held by the Croatoan werowance for a while." She brushed away a pesky fly buzzing about her face. "But these days it is held by none other than . . . Chief Powhatan!"

"Really?" he cried, his mood soaring. Even his injured shoulder seemed to ache less all of a sudden. "But that is incredible!"

"I know." Liz grinned. "But it is true. Matachanna has seen it many times. She told a story of her sister Matoaka trying on the enormous headdress as a tiny child and staggering about the village with it. She thinks that may be when her father first gave Matoaka the nickname Pocahontas, which means something like "Little Mischief"—Matachanna wasn't sure of the exact translation."

"Gilbert must have found out somehow that the headdress was now with the Powhatan," Sam mused.

"Oh, yes, I almost forgot that part," Liz said. "Matachanna says Captain Smith would have seen the headdress on numerous occasions during meetings with Chief Powhatan. He could have described it to Gilbert, or it is also possible that one of those meetings was public enough for Gilbert to attend."

Sam smiled. "Yes," he said. "And he figured out a way

to turn it into a clue. What a coincidence that the verse worked out so well!"

"Not so much a coincidence," Liz pointed out, her voice suddenly tinged with sadness. "Just very clever on Gilbert's part. Too bad he was lost in the Starving Time—I would have very much liked to meet him."

"Me, too." Sam glanced toward the Martin house, where he was sure Liz's father was waiting to assign him that day's tasks. "But we can honor his memory now by solving the puzzle he so carefully laid for his cousins." He thought for a moment. "Do you suppose Matachanna could figure out a way for me to see that headdress?"

"I don't know." Liz sounded dubious. "She has seen it many times, but mostly at a distance, so she wasn't certain of all the details. But she promised to try to get a better look and report back as soon as possible."

Sam swallowed back a sigh of impatience. Now that the next clue was so close, he could hardly stand the suspense. What would the headdress reveal? He couldn't imagine.

Then another thought occurred to him. "Do you suppose the headdress itself might be the treasure?" he asked. "If it's anywhere near as valuable as one of King James's crowns . . ."

Liz was already shaking her head. "Matachanna described it to me," she said. "It's nothing like an English crown. It's made of materials such as deerskin, feathers— that sort of thing. No really valuable bits at all, from what she said."

"All right. It must be another clue, then." Sam bit his lip and glanced at her. "Do you think we should keep this from Hal, at least for the moment? I haven't told you what he was up to in the fort last night. . . ."

He quickly told her about Hal stealing the letter. By the time he finished, Liz's expression was outraged. "That rat!" she cried. "I am sorry to have him as a relation. How could he betray you that way?"

"Never mind, no harm done. He never reached Jasper with it." Sam had already moved on from the incident in his own mind. "But as I said, we may want to wait a while to tell him about the headdress. He has a big mouth, and we don't want to take chances."

"Agreed," Liz said. "I won't breathe a word of this to Hal until we know more. I shall even force myself to wait before I scold him for his absolute foolishness."

Liz said good-bye and headed off to the vegetable plot

while Sam went into the house. He nearly ran into Hal in the office doorway.

"Pardon me," Sam mumbled, feeling a twinge of guilt. Fortunately, it appeared that Hal had just risen from bed; he merely mumbled something in an irritated tone and moved on without noticing Sam's troubled expression.

Late that afternoon Sam finished his work and prepared to head for home. He looked around to say good-bye to Liz, but she was nowhere to be seen. Much to his relief, however, Hal was absent as well—it had been a struggle to avoid meeting his eye all day for fear of giving away his thoughts. Deciding not to press his luck, Sam headed back across the fields toward the fort.

He'd barely passed through the gate when he heard a great hue and cry from somewhere near the center of the settlement. Curious, he walked that way to see what was happening.

He found a crowd gathered in the street near the governor's house. Pushing his way through, he craned his neck to see. But it was no use. Taller men blocked his view. Spotting Red, the lanky young man he'd met on the voyage over, he quickly made his way toward him.

"What is happening?" he asked.

Red grabbed him, looking excited. "It is your brother William," he exclaimed. "He is accused of robbing the home of Governor Gates!"

Twelve

"What?" Sam exclaimed. He laughed uncertainly. "What do you mean?"

Red gestured toward the governor's house. It stood at one side of the central square; it was larger than most of the houses in the fort and grander than any other building aside from the church. "Governor Gates noticed that some important document was missing from his office. A horseshoe was found lying in the room, and when the governor's servants went to the blacksmith shop, they found the paper amongst William's things." His eyes shone with some emotion halfway between fear and glee. "Sir Dale says William must hang for it!"

Sam's heart sank, and a terrible feeling of déjà vu filled his body with a shame that felt like molten lead in his veins. Could this really be happening again? Was the Gates family name to be tarnished anew? He and William had come to the New World to *escape* this sort of thing. . . . He pushed his way to the front of the crowd that filled the square, ignoring the choking dust that hung in the air from the movement of so many feet, as well as the jostling that stressed his sore shoulder.

William was standing in the square directly before the governor's house, still dressed in his soot-smudged work clothes. His face was pale and his mouth set in a grim line as he faced a group of some half dozen gentlemen from the colony's leadership. At the front of this group was the governor himself, who was glowering at William with arms crossed over his chest. Sir Thomas Dale was beside him. Until now, Sam had seen the marshall of Virginia only from a distance, though he had heard tales around the settlement of his quick temper and strict enforcement of the code of laws and behavior that everyone called Dale's Code. Now that he had a closer look at his deep scowl and pitiless expression, Sam had no trouble believing even the direst of those stories.

"Do you realize the importance of what you stole, young man?" Dale was shouting at William. He held up a small, slim silver case and waived it around. "The Second Virginia Charter is perhaps the most important document in this settlement. Stealing it is akin to treason!"

145

"Please," Sam blurted, unable to hold himself back. He had to talk to his brother—see what was really going on. "William, what's this about?"

William turned toward him, his face twisted with confusion. "Samuel," he cried. "Tell them it's not true. Tell them I am not a thief!"

"Silence!" Dale thundered.

"Wait." The governor raised a hand to silence his deputy. His grim expression softened slightly as he looked at Sam. "Let him talk to his brother. Perhaps he can pull a confession out of him."

"Confession or no, we cannot allow this crime to stand," Dale said sternly. But he backed up a few steps.

At the governor's nod, Sam rushed to William. "What happened?" he asked, trying to keep his voice low enough to escape the curious ears of the onlookers. "How did that document get into your possession?"

"I know not." William's eyes were anguished. "They say they found it with my belongings, but I know nothing of how it got there!"

Sam bit his lip. His brother was far from perfect. But he had never, to Sam's knowledge, been a thief.

"You can help me through this, can't you, Sam?" William stared at him pleadingly.

Seeing his older brother brought so low twisted Sam's heart painfully. He wasn't used to William being the helpless one. William was the one who'd protected the younger, smaller, physically weaker Sam all through childhood. But now the tide had turned. Now it was William who needed help. But what could Sam do?

Keeping his concerns to himself, Sam gave his brother a pat on the arm. "I need to think about what to do. Try not to worry. I'll figure out something."

He took a few steps, willing his brain to work. He might not have William's brawn but there had to be some way for him to work through this problem. As he glanced around for inspiration, he noticed a figure peering out from around the corner of the next building. Moving a little closer, his eyes grew wide. Jasper!

Jasper spotted him at the same moment. His thin lips stretched into a smirk.

Without pausing to think about what he was doing, Sam raced around the corner and flung himself upon the older man. "You had something to do with this, didn't you?" he cried, pummeling Jasper's chest and neck with both fists. "Why don't you deal with me and leave my brother out of it?"

"I *tried* to do so." Jasper, who was taller and stronger than Sam, easily fended off the attack. He then gave Sam a sound cuff on the side of the head that sent him spinning away, dizzy and disoriented. "But you keep insisting on surviving." Striding forward, he grabbed Sam by the throat, lifting him off the ground against the side of the building. Sam struggled against his grip, but it was no use. He felt his breath being cut off as he gasped vainly for air.

"Oi! What's happening here?"

Sam was always glad to hear Liz's voice, but never so much as at that moment. She marched straight up to Jasper and gave him a slap on the cheek. Jasper was so startled that he dropped Sam, who immediately staggered out of reach.

"Mind your business, girl," Jasper snarled.

"He framed William," Sam choked out, rubbing his throat. "He set it up so the governor thinks William stole a valuable document out of his home."

Liz gasped, which merely made Jasper smile more. "Perhaps you ought to hand over that treasure map now, before anyone else gets hurt." He slid his eyes over to Liz, looking her up and down. "For instance, I'd hate to see you or your lovely lady friend come to any harm."

Sam gulped, realizing that they were out of sight of the rest of the settlers. But the thought had barely formed in his mind when they heard rapid footsteps coming their way. A moment later, the governor himself rushed around the corner.

He stopped short at the sight of the trio. "Young Gates," he said brusquely, "I wish you'd talk some sense into that brother of yours. Things will go much easier for him if he confesses."

"Governor Gates!" Hal raced around the corner after him, red-faced and out of breath. "I need to speak with you."

"Not now." The governor didn't even bother to glance Hal's way. He was still glaring at Sam with a disapproving frown. Sam lowered his eyes, feeling awful. So much for improving the Gates family reputation in the New World . . .

"Please, Governor!" Hal insisted. "There has been a terrible mistake. William Gates didn't steal that document!"

Sam blinked at him in surprise, but Hal didn't look at him. He was staring earnestly at the governor, who had finally turned to face him.

149

"What are you on about, boy?" he demanded, sounding impatient. "If you've information on the crime, spit it out, else I'll have you thrown in prison as well."

Hal looked nervous, but he kept talking. "I was walking by your house, sir, and I witnessed the whole thing through the window," he said, the words coming rapidly. "One of your servants was walking by and accidentally knocked the document case to the floor with her elbow and then left the room without noticing she'd done so. A few moments later the blacksmith's mutt came in carrying a horseshoe in its jaws. It dropped the shoe and grabbed the silver case, then made off with it." He finally paused long enough to take a deep, albeit shaky breath. "The dog must've dropped your case in William Gates's things when it returned to the forge."

Sam narrowed his eyes, trying to deduce whether Hal was telling the truth. Like everyone else in the settlement, he'd seen the blacksmith's black-and-white dog wandering about the fort at will. It *did* have a reputation for trouble, though its usual targets were edible stuff and leather goods, not horseshoes and silver cases.

The governor looked dubious as well. "So you are telling me the blacksmith's dog is the thief?" He crossed his arms over his chest. "If you truly witnessed all this, you'll be able to tell me precisely where the document case was before it was knocked to the floor, then."

"Of course, sir," Hal replied without hesitation. "It was upon a small table against the wall to the right of the fireplace."

"That's correct." The governor paused, stroking his reddish brown beard and staring at Hal. "Your tale is a bit far-fetched. . . ."

"But it must be true," Sam put in, unable to keep quiet any longer. "Please, sir. You must know that my brother is no thief. And he respects you far too much to ever do you wrong."

"Hmm." The governor still didn't look convinced.

"I will vouch for William Gates, too," Liz spoke up. "I have spoken with him enough to know that his heart is true and honest. Such a man would not do what he's being accused of, sir."

Sam glanced at her, a little unnerved by the passion in her voice. For a moment he wondered if that same passion would exist if he, not William, were in trouble. Shaking off the inappropriate thought, Sam gazed at the governor and waited. Silence descended upon the group, and Sam was sure the others could hear the rapid beating of his heart. Finally, the governor's expression relaxed slightly.

"You are Martin's elder daughter, yes?" he asked Liz.

Liz straightened up to her full height. "I am."

"With all due respect, Governor, this is ridiculous." Sam had nearly forgotten that Jasper was still there until he spoke. "Are we to believe a *dog* stole one of the most valuable documents in Jamestown? You all but caught that Gates fellow red-handed."

The governor surveyed Jasper. "And who might you be, sir?"

Jasper gave his name. "I came over on the ship with William Gates. I found him to be nothing but a trouble-maker."

"What?" Sam cried, indignation bubbling over. "Please, Governor! It was quite the contrary. Jasper was the one who—"

"Enough!" the governor ordered, holding up a hand. "I am not interested in petty squabbles." He squared his shoulders and nodded toward Hal. "In light of this eyewitness, I shall release William Gates . . . at least for now." He turned to address Sam. "But you may wish to advise your brother that we shall all be keeping an eye on him from here out. He'll want to work extra hard and keep his nose clean if he wishes to regain his good name in this colony."

"Thank you, sir." Sam felt limp with relief. "I'll be sure to tell him."

Jasper muttered an oath under his breath and stalked off. A moment later, the governor turned and left as well.

"Whew!" Sam exclaimed when they were both out of earshot. "That was something." Glancing over at Hal, he stuck out his hand. "Thank you. I am grateful to you for speaking up."

Hal shrugged, ignoring the outstretched hand. "I only did it because your brother doesn't deserve the noose," he muttered. "Not when *I'm* the one who took that blasted document case."

"What?" Liz cried, her hand flying to her mouth. "*You* stole it? Why on earth would you do such a thing?"

"It was that Jasper fellow's plan," Hal said sullenly. "Said he'd cut me in for a full fifty percent, he did. What else could I do?"

Sam was in shock. Was no one in this blasted colony to

be trusted. "So you *did* go to Jasper, even after I stopped you last night? How could you do that?"

"The same way you could try to keep your latest news of the treasure from me," Hal retorted with a scowl. "Don't play innocent. I saw you whispering with my sister this morning. Trying to cut me out, weren't you?"

"We weren't!" Liz cried.

Sam shook his head, his sense of outrage growing as he thought of what Hal and Jasper had put William through. His poor brother had done nothing wrong, and yet he would still be punished. True, he would not hang, but the accusing glares and distrust might be worse. Sam knew how much his brother had hoped for a fresh start and a clear name. But was that hope gone because of Hal? Anger flared in Sam's chest. "Can you blame us for not trusting you?" he exclaimed, clenching his fists at his side. "You have to confess to what you did. That's the only way to clear William's name for good and all."

"Not on your life," Hal replied immediately.

Liz grabbed him by the arm. "Sam is right," she said. "You must tell the governor the truth!"

Hal shook her off. "Are you feeble?" he said. "I won't

sacrifice myself for some blacksmith's assistant. It's not as if anyone important cares about a common laborer's good name, anyway."

"*I* care!" Sam yelled. "And if you won't confess, I'll tell the governor myself?"

"Will you, then?" Hal glared at him. "Then I suppose we'll have to see which carries more weight—the *coincidence* of your surname, or the weight of my father's good name and years of service to this colony."

Sam bit his lip. Hal had a point. Despite the governor's interest in his namesakes, Sam wasn't sure that would be enough to sway him to the right side—especially now, when the Gates name was in such disgrace.

He could do nothing more than watch as Hal walked off without a backward glance. Now, more than ever, Sam wanted that treasure.

The next two or three days passed very slowly. There was no further word from Matachanna; Liz hadn't seen any sign of her since their last meeting. In the meantime, Sam was doing his best to avoid Hal, though that proved challenging at times. It was a bit easier to stay away from Jasper, who was being kept very busy at the new well site.

Finally, one morning, Sam arrived for work to find Liz once again perched on the edge of the water trough waiting for him. "I saw her," she greeted him without preamble.

"Matachanna?" Sam glanced around to ascertain that no one else was within earshot. "What did she say? Did she get a closer look at that headdress?"

His heart fell when he noticed that Liz looked rather grim. "I saw her only briefly at our meeting spot early this morning," she reported. "She said she did manage to sneak into Powhatan's longhouse the day of our previous meeting. However, she had barely approached the headdress when her father came in and caught her. She refused to tell him what she was doing there and was soundly punished for it. The women of the tribe have been keeping a close eye on her ever since, and that is why she wasn't able to come for so long. Today was the first time she was able to slip away."

Sam felt worse and worse with every one of Liz's words. He hated the thought that his quest for this mysterious treasure was getting people in trouble—first William, and now Matachanna. And for what? They were no closer to the answer or the treasure than before; at least it felt that way. . . .

Just then a maidservant came in search of Liz to help with the day's baking. "We can finish discussing this later," Liz said as she left. She reached out and touched his arm with a small smile. "Try not to worry."

"All right." Sam watched her go, feeling a slight tingle upon his arm even after she had removed her hand.

Then he turned and stared into the murky water of the trough beside him, wondering what to do next. He didn't want to give up—now that he'd had a taste of the treasure hunt, it was all he could think of most of the time. He couldn't imagine giving it up now. But he also couldn't imagine continuing to allow his quest to hurt those he cared about.

When he looked up again, he saw William walking across the fields carrying a heavy set of plow blades as if they weighed no more than Sam's notebook. "Morning, brother," William greeted him. "Taking a drink from the livestock trough, are you?"

The words were lighthearted, but William's smile didn't quite reach his eyes. He had been rather downcast since the incident with the document case. Seeing him still looking that way made Sam feel worse than ever.

"I have your master's plow parts ready." William dropped the iron he was carrying on the ground. "Is he at home?"

"Er . . ." Sam didn't answer for a moment, still lost in thought. He wondered if it was time to share the secret of the treasure with his brother. Perhaps he should have done so long ago.

Suddenly, a cacophony of cries rang out from the back of the house. "What's that?" William asked, looking in that direction.

"Fire!" a woman screamed.

Without a word, the Gates brothers raced around the house to the cooking area at the back and rushed inside. Sam gasped and stopped short when he saw what was happening. Liz's skirt was on fire!

Liz was screaming and spinning in circles in front of the big cooking fireplace, the smoke from the burning fabric rising about her like a shroud. As Sam watched, Mrs. Martin beat at the flames with a broom. But her efforts were in vain as the fire greedily swallowed up more and more of the long, thick fabric.

The maidservant let out another scream punctuated by coughs. Smoke was billowing out and filling the small room.

Sam stood rooted in horror, unable to react, while in front of him, Liz burned.

Thirteen

"**S**tand aside!" William shouted, springing into action.

He raced forward, grabbing Liz with both hands. He slung her over his shoulder and ran forward through the main part of the house. Sparks and ashes flew out behind him, threatening to light the entire house afire, but William didn't pause.

The maidservant stayed behind, stomping out the little flares. But Sam and Mrs. Martin ran after William and Liz. Sam's head was spinning. What was William going to do? As soon as the last bits of Liz's dress and shift were burnt away, there would be nothing at all protecting her tender skin from the flames. . . .

They all burst outside. William's steps never slowed until he'd reached the edge of the largest water trough in front of the house. Then he skidded to a stop and dropped Liz right in, being careful to protect her head from the hard stone side with his hand. There was a loud sizzle and a great

whoosh of black smoke. But a moment later, the fire was out and Liz was safe from harm.

"What's going on out here?" Mr. Martin stomped out of the house, a sheaf of papers in one hand. "I'm trying to work, yet people are running through my house like a herd of—" He stopped short at the sight of Liz in the water trough. The papers fluttered to the ground. "Oh, my!"

His wife, sobbing with relief, told him what had happened. ". . . and this man's strength and quick thinking saved her life!" she finished, rushing over and throwing her arms about William, who, now that it was all over, looked rather sheepish.

"'Twas nothing, madam," he said. "Any man would have done the same."

William's words stung Sam a bit. Any man would have—but what had Sam himself done but stood there like a fool watching Liz burn? He pushed such thoughts aside. Liz was alive. That should be all that mattered.

Climbing out of the trough, Liz winced. The wet and tattered remains of her skirt clung to her, and her face was pale and streaked with soot. Sam fought back an urge to rub the dirt from her cheek.

"Thank you, William," Liz said, tears streaming down

her face. "Thank you ever so much."

"Indeed." Her father still looked rather stunned, but he reached out and grasped William's hand, shaking it firmly. "I owe you a debt of gratitude, son. I know you've had your troubles lately. Be certain that I'll let the governor know of your courage and quick wit—that should go a long way toward restoring your name in this town."

Sam shot his brother a warm smile. But on the inside, his brain raced. Would it be enough to redeem William in the eyes of the colony? And what would this mean for him and Elizabeth?

Luckily, the news of William's heroics spread through the settlement faster than the flames through Liz's skirt. By day's end everyone seemed to know what had happened.

At their evening meal, William was in a better mood than Sam had seen in days. That was the good news. The bad news was that through the whole meal he couldn't seem to stop talking about Liz.

"You know, I'd conversed with her a time or two before," he told Sam. "But until today I never really noticed what a spirited, attractive girl she is." He smiled confidently. "Once

I'm a bit more established, I think I shall see about making her my wife. It would be a good match, would it not? Not only would she be a pleasing companion, but her father is a gentleman with an established plantation. Aye, a union with Elizabeth Martin makes good sense, to be sure."

Sam choked down a bite of food. "Er, perhaps," he said, doing his best to keep his consternation out of his voice. "Then again, there are a number of equally eligible young ladies in the colony. No sense in setting your mind on one at this early date."

"To the contrary." William tapped his spoon on the table. "Thinking of a fine future with a lovely young lady will give me all the more will to succeed. I see no reason that lovely lady should be anyone but Elizabeth."

Sam wanted to speak up, to protest. After all, he'd met Liz first. If any Gates brother were to court her one day, it should be he.

But he didn't say any of that. He still felt guilt over what had happened with Jasper and the governor's document, not to mention the fact that he still hadn't told William about the treasure. Besides, if not for William, Liz might not be alive this day at all. How could he argue against that?

He stared down at his food with no appetite, feeling like the world's worst brother as well as its greatest coward.

The next morning a light drizzle soaked the fields and hid the sun as Sam walked to the Martins'. He had barely set to work when Liz found him in the otherwise deserted office. Despite all that had happened, even seeing her there before him lifted his mood just as it always did.

"Good morning," he said, hoping his feelings had not crept into his voice. "How are you?"

"A little better." Liz glanced down at her right hand, which was bandaged. "I'm forbidden from cooking until my burns are fully healed. I only have this tiny spot on my hand, though as you can see, mother has wrapped every bit of linen she had around it. And then, of course, there are a few burns on my legs as well." She coughed. "Blasted cough! The smoke still seems trapped within me. In any case, I suppose I should be grateful for the holiday."

Sam smiled. "We are quite the pair—I with my wound, you with your burns. But, it is good to see you in such fine spirits."

"Indeed." Liz smiled back. "I have your brother to thank

for that. And my father was as good as his word—he's been telling all who will listen what your brother did. Why, I heard from the governor's kitchen girl that William has been invited to stand sentry with Sir Dale himself. How do you like that? It seems William is making his way up in the world."

"He will enjoy standing sentry," Sam said, trying not to notice how her eyes sparkled as she spoke of his brother. "William has always liked playing with firearms. Manning the cannons will suit his fancy all the more."

Liz laughed, though it soon turned into another cough. "Yes, he is certainly a man in the mold of such as Captain Smith or others of that sort. A man bold of thought and of action."

Sam busied himself with some papers as an excuse not to respond for a moment. He was trying to hold back the tide of resentment rising within him, but it wasn't easy. First William had announced his intentions to make Liz his wife. And now it was looking as though she might not find such advances at all unwelcome.

And no wonder, he thought, feeling quite sorry for himself. *What woman wouldn't prefer a man of action over a coward who is afraid to act at all? If only I could somehow prove to her that I'm no more a coward than my brother . . .*

"But never mind all that," Liz said. "I was hoping you could distract me from the pain of my burns with talk of the treasure."

Sam sighed. "What is there to talk of?" he said, feeling nearly as discouraged by the new topic as the previous one. "Matachanna didn't find anything and got punished for her trouble. I won't ask her to do that again."

"I know how you feel." Liz grimaced as she carefully perched upon the edge of her chair, keeping as much of her legs as possible from touching it. "I only wish I could get a look at that headdress myself. Perhaps there'd be something Matachanna didn't notice." Her eyes lit up. "I know! Perhaps if she could find out when her father might wear it next, we could sneak into the village and spy . . ." Her words trailed off, and she sighed. "Or perhaps not. It would be dreadfully risky."

"No, but that's it!" Sam suddenly dropped the papers he was holding and stood bolt upright. He knew exactly what he had to do to move forward on the treasure hunt—*and* to prove to Liz that he was no coward. Ignoring the doubts and fears already trying to crowd into his mind, he smiled at Liz. "Never mind waiting for Powhatan to wear it. That would take too long. No, I'm going to sneak into his house and get a look at that headdress myself!"

Fourteen

Unfortunately, Sam's declaration was not met with the enthusiasm he had anticipated. "What?" Liz shrilled in disbelief. "Powhatan was angry enough to find his own daughter lurking about in his house. What do you think would happen to you if he were to catch you?"

"He will not catch me," Sam said with more confidence than he felt. "It is the only way."

He expected her to argue further. Instead, she nodded.

"All right," she said. "But if you're going, I'm going, too."

From the stubborn tilt of her chin, Sam knew arguing was out of the question. So very early the next morning, both of them found themselves waiting in a secluded spot for Matachanna to appear. She smiled shyly when she saw Sam there. But the smile vanished when Liz and Sam told her of their latest plan.

"Oh, but that could mean death—and not just for the

both of you!" she cried in her accented English. "My father is angry with your people lately. There was the fight with your leader Ratcliffe, and chief De La Warr's many raids upon our villages these last several years, the burning of our cornfields and the killing of our people." Her face was sad as she spoke. "There was even the way my sister Matoaka was told that her friend John Smith was dead, when we later learned he had really sailed for your homeland. Matoaka pined so that my father nearly wiped out your village then. Such a thing as you are suggesting could be all it takes to push him to that decision after all."

Sam gulped, realizing that what she said was probably true. He'd heard mutterings around the colony about the touchy and often violent relations between settlers and natives. If he decided to go through with his plan, he might not just be risking his own life and Liz's, but those of every Englishman in Jamestown and the surrounding plantations.

Still, he couldn't back down now.

"I will be careful," he assured Matachanna. "I know I can do this. I *must* do this, or we will have no chance of ever finding that treasure."

"Don't you mean *we* must do this?" Liz reminded him, stifling a cough. "I am coming with you, remember?"

Matachanna twisted a leaf from a nearby bush in her hand, her dark eyes anxious. "Please," she said. "If you do insist on attempting this, one might be safer than two."

"She's right," Liz said promptly. "I'll go. I am smaller and can be quieter."

Sam shook his head. "That may be true," he said. "But it is my keen memory that can carry the information back for all of us. Besides, you still have that cough from the fire. It could give you away."

Liz opened her mouth as if to protest, then closed it again. "You are right," she said simply. "You shall be the one to go."

Two days later the plan was put in motion. Matachanna had convinced Sam to wait that long because she had heard her father would be leaving then for one of the many other villages under his rule. Sam had been impatient at the delay, but had agreed that it was worth it; the risk would be much less with Powhatan absent. It had also given his injured shoulder more time to heal; he would need all the strength and agility he had to sneak in and out of the village.

Finally the day arrived. As quietly as possible, Sam and Liz made their way through the forest on the far side of the river, following the directions Matachanna had given them. Sam had been concerned about Liz walking so far with her burns, but she had assured him that they barely troubled her anymore. And indeed, the one on her hand looked much better already. He hadn't dared admit to himself, but the other reason he had wanted Liz to stay home was fear. If he messed this up and she bore witness, it would only serve to make William that much more appealing.

"Matachanna said to look for a tree with a face like an old man," Sam said, breaking the comfortable silence of their walk. "What does that mean? What tree has a face?"

"There!" Liz pointed to a gnarled, pitted trunk nearby. "That must be the tree."

Sam cocked his head and squinted. It *vaguely* resembled a man. . . . Shrugging, he followed her. "Before we go much farther, you should start looking for a hiding spot. You ought not to get so close that you might encounter any of Powhatan's peo—"

"Oh!" Liz gasped, cutting Sam off in midsentence.

Sam spun around, fearing the worst. Had some native

sentry spotted them? Could Jasper possibly have noticed them leaving the settlement and followed them out here to try and finish Sam off for good?

Instead he saw Matachanna standing there. "I am sorry to surprise you," she said to Liz. "I am glad you did not scream." She glanced around and lowered her voice. "I have bad news. My father did not leave on his journey yesterday as he had intended. My sister Matoaka was found sneaking to a new plantation being made by your people upriver from here, and he was so angry that he delayed his trip to scold her. He left only an hour ago."

Sam guessed that the plantation in question was the one being started by John Rolfe, the dark-haired settler who kept telling everyone he was going to make his fortune in tobacco. For someone like Matoaka—curious about all colonists—the temptation would be hard to resist. Shaking his head, he moved a step closer to Matachanna. "But your father is gone now, is he not?" he asked.

She nodded. "I wish you would not try this plan. It is dangerous for you."

"We'll be all right," Sam assured her, briefly touching Isaac's ring, a habit he'd developed that seemed to provide a bit of added courage when needed. "I am ready for this."

And indeed he was. Now that the hour was here, he felt nothing but calm certainty. It was almost as if everything in his life had been leading up to this moment. This was when he would prove that he was indeed a man, worthy of whatever treasure he might find. Perhaps this was the moment he would look back on someday, the very moment when the compass point of his life would once again swing in the right direction.

Throwing back his shoulders, Sam nodded toward the path, and the three of them resumed their walk. A short while later they found themselves close enough to smell the smoke of the village's fires. Silently, Matachanna melted away into the forest while Liz found a hiding spot in the shadow of a rocky outcropping on the bank of a creek. In a whisper, she promised to wait there while Sam completed his task.

His two compatriots safely out of the way, Sam walked on alone. He crept through the trees, his eyes scanning the area frantically. He'd already seen how Matachanna could appear as if out of nowhere; her bronze skin and tawny clothing helped her blend in with the shifting shadows of the tree trunks and rocks of the forest. Sam didn't want to be surprised by an unexpected native sentry before he had even made it to the camp.

He found the native village just where Matachanna had said it would be. The trickiest part was getting inside their high fence made of narrow tree branches. It encircled all the houses and then wrapped back around itself like a snake, leaving only a narrow passage into the village. A young native man crouched on his heels near this entrance, making marks in the dirt with a stick and looking rather bored. The sentry.

Doing as Matachanna had advised, Sam hid behind a tree and waited. A few minutes passed, giving him just enough time to wonder if Matachanna had changed her mind about playing her part—a part that had been inspired by Liz's recent accident. Matachanna was going to pretend to almost get burned, and in the process, she would set a few baskets or other small items afire in a spot far from the chief's longhouse. They all figured that should keep the rest of the natives busy long enough for Sam to slip in and then out again without being seen.

Suddenly, a scream rose from the far end of the village.

Even though Sam was expecting it, he jumped slightly.

The native sentry was startled, too. He dropped his stick and raced into the village. From within rose cries of alarm.

Sam didn't hesitate; he raced in after the sentry. Once inside the fence, he immediately spotted the longhouse Matachanna had described. It was the largest and finest in the village, as befitted Powhatan's rank.

Glancing around to make sure he hadn't been spotted, he ducked inside. A single fire was burning in the center, its smoke trailing lazily upward to a hole in the roof overhead.

Sam looked around, his eyes wide with curiosity. Most of the settlers back in Jamestown spoke of the natives as if they were little better than animals. But the chief's house, built soundly of poles and bark, was every bit as comfortable as the wattle-and-daub homes the Englishmen had built for themselves. The home was airy and spacious— much more so than the humble room Sam and William shared in the Jamestown barracks. There were sleeping benches lined with luxurious animal pelts along the wall; neat fire pits beneath each roof opening; and cooking utensils, weapons, woven mats, and preserved food hanging on the walls or the beams overhead. It was, despite all word to the contrary, homey and comfortable.

Dragging his gaze from the inviting sleeping benches, Sam noticed an elaborate headdress hanging on a rack at the far end of the longhouse. Quickly, he made his way toward it. When he was inches away, he carefully reached up and lifted it down. It was surprisingly heavy, and Sam felt his sore shoulder protest. Ignoring the stab, he placed the headdress on the ground near the fire and kneeled down for a closer look.

The headdress was simple, but beautiful. It consisted of a tanned animal hide decorated with shells, feathers, and bits of copper. The main part was dyed in a simple pattern of dark brown and red, with a stylized design at its center that resembled a crooked arrow with a circle around its tip.

Sam's heart sank as he stared at it. Somehow he'd been expecting that as soon as he set eyes on the headdress, he would know what clue Gilbert had intended to be seen. But the truth was, he had no better idea now than he did before he entered the longhouse.

He reached out to turn it over—perhaps there was

something more on the back. But just as his fingers brushed the worn leather, he heard a sharp whistle. Sam's heart began to race. That was the signal he and Matachanna had agreed on earlier. Someone was coming!

Fifteen

Sam hurriedly scooped up the headdress and hung it back in its spot, hoping it looked the same as before. Then he turned and raced for the only door.

Too late! He saw the shadow of someone just outside the doorway. With a gasp, he dove to one side, burrowing into a pile of animal skins.

A second later, the sound of heavy footsteps entered the room. Peeking out from under the skins, Sam's eyes widened as he saw Chief Powhatan. He was followed by several other warriors, including the one Hal had said was the chief's brother. All of them quickly gathered around the fire, speaking in loud, angry voices in their native tongue.

Sam didn't dare move, though his mind was racing. Matachanna's warnings ran through his head, along with the ghastly tales he'd heard back in London and those since arriving. John Smith had nearly been clubbed to death when Powhatan's men had first taken him captive. And John

Ratcliffe, captain of one of the original ships that had settled the island, had reportedly been tortured to death by the tribe's women.

Then he thought of Liz waiting for him in the forest. If they caught him, surely they would soon find her, too. He couldn't let that happen. He'd failed to save her once already; he wouldn't do it again.

With new resolve, he lifted the skin again and peered out at the men. Perhaps they had finished their discussion and would soon leave.

But instead, more native warriors poured into the long-house. All of them appeared angry and excited, though the anger seemed not to be directed at one another. Sam wished he understood their language so he would know what had happened to bring the chief back so abruptly. Had there been some further skirmish against his own people? Or, had his presence been noticed?

As he wriggled slightly, trying for a better look, he felt his arm touch some hard object nestled within the animal skins. Moving carefully and staying as silent as possible, he felt for it. At first he thought it was a small rock, though when he glanced down at it he saw that it was actually the skull of some small animal, a rabbit or perhaps a squirrel.

He measured the distance to the doorway, knowing he would have only one chance at this. No new men had entered for a moment or two; all were now gathered about the fire arguing loudly with one another.

Sam's fingers tightened around the animal skull. Then, not allowing himself to overthink what he was doing, he reached one arm out from beneath the skins and hurled the skull toward the doorway.

It flew out cleanly, landing with a soft thud in the dirt and then clattering against something outside.

Several of the men at the fire heard the noise and spun around. There was a new flurry of discussion. A moment later, all of them, including the chief, ran out the door.

Sam raced after them, his heart in his throat. The men hadn't gone far, but when he peered out the door, their backs were to him. More natives were hurrying toward them; he prayed they were still too far away to notice him as he slipped through the doorway and around the side of the longhouse.

He was out of sight—for the moment, at least. Pressing his back against the rough bark exterior, he glanced around to measure his chances. True, he had made it out of one tight spot, but he still needed to find a way to the village's only exit unnoticed.

His heart racing, Sam peered around the corner of the building. Some of the warriors were starting to head back into the longhouse. Others, however, were striding toward the passage in the fence. Sam's heart sank. How long could he stay out of sight?

Just then, he spotted Matachanna among the gathered natives. She wore a worried expression as she glanced nervously around.

That gave Sam an idea. Pursing his lips, he did his best to imitate the bird-call whistle he'd heard her do earlier. Several of the natives glanced curiously around at the sound, but Matachanna's eyes widened immediately. She cried out, gesturing for others to follow as if she'd spotted something at the back end of the village, then raced in that direction— away from Sam's hiding place.

As soon as Sam saw the last of the warriors follow her, clutching their spears grimly, he darted into the open. His back tingled with the feeling that, at any moment, it could be pierced by a tossed spear or half a dozen arrows. But he kept running, dashing out through the narrow entranceway and flinging himself to his belly beneath the closest clump of shrubbery.

It took a few minutes for his heart to stop pounding. In that time, several native warriors came out and stood at the entrance in the fence, but though they peered suspiciously about, they did not spot Sam. After a while, he was able to ease himself carefully back into the thicker growth until, finally, he made his escape through the trees.

Moments later he was at the outcropping where he'd left Liz. "Liz?" he hissed. "Where are you? We need to get out of here—fast."

There was no answer but for the soft chittering of a squirrel in a nearby tree. Sam felt his entire body go cold. What had happened to Liz?

Frantically, he raced all the way around the rocky creek bed, splashing through the water without caring that his shoes were instantly soaked. His heart was pounding and his mouth was dry. Perhaps this was the reason for Powhatan's return; perhaps he'd found Liz! If she'd been captured, Sam would never forgive himself. For a moment he was ready to race back to the native village, to demand that they take him prisoner in her place.

But he forced himself to stop and think. Liz was clever; surely she hadn't been so foolish as to get captured. Besides, he'd seen no sign of her while he was hiding in the village. Perhaps she'd heard the commotion or seen Powhatan go by and decided to move to a safer spot.

He retraced their steps from earlier, walking softly and staring around in all directions. Every time a bird flitted up through the sun-dappled woods or a tiny creature rustled in the underbrush, he felt his heart leap and then plummet again. Where was she?

He was focusing so hard that he didn't hear the even softer footsteps creeping up behind him—not until a pair of arms locked around his throat. He cried out in terror and spun around.

"Sam!" Liz sobbed, hugging him tightly around the neck. "I was sure they'd captured you!"

His pounding heart slowed—at least a little. He'd never been so close to Liz before. Staring into her eyes, he swallowed hard.

"I thought the same of you," he said, his voice squeaking in the middle of the sentence in a rather embarrassing manner.

Suddenly aware of their tight embrace, Liz released her grip on him and backed quickly away. Small pink spots appeared on her pale cheeks. "I'm sorry if I startled you," she said, not quite meeting his eye. "I was just so relieved . . ."

"Er, yes." Sam cleared his throat and stared down at the ground for a moment, trying to regain his composure. "I am glad to see you. When you were not at the hiding spot, I feared the worst."

"I saw Chief Powhatan and his men go by, heading for the village," she explained. "I thought being that close might no longer be safe, so I sought out a better spot." She glanced around, looking nervous. "Speaking of which, perhaps it would be prudent to put some distance between us and the natives now."

As they hurried back toward Jamestown, Sam told her how he had escaped. He also described what he'd seen of the headdress. Thanks to his excellent memory, he'd retained every detail, and as he walked he paused to record it by sketching it out in his notebook. Still, neither he nor Liz had any idea what it might mean.

"Perhaps we are on the wrong track," Liz said with a sigh as they came within sight of the settlement on the opposite bank of the river. "The verse might not refer to that headdress at all."

"You may be right." Sam stared down at the notebook page. It was all so disheartening; they would need to start over and think of other possibilities for the clue. But something about that crooked-arrow design tugged at his mind. Why did it look familiar? For once, his memory failed him, and he sighed and tucked the notebook away.

Over the next three days Sam continued to think about the treasure clues whenever possible. He also discovered the source of the natives' consternation; there had been another skirmish in the ongoing hostilities between Powhatan's people and the Englishmen. Several settlers had been injured and the fields of one plantation burned. Many were talking retaliation, and the governor had called for extra sentries in the fort, which kept William away from home at night.

One morning he came in keyed up and excited. "You should've been there, brother," he told Sam, who was pulling on his clothes for the day. "The savages were at the edge of the wood, looking over at us. We saw them right away, of course. Sir Dale said if they came any closer we'd have to turn Edward and John upon them!"

"Edward and John?" Sam repeated sleepily, wondering which settlers his brother meant. He knew several Johns, but the only Edward he'd met was a boy of around ten.

William laughed heartily. "Of course! You probably wouldn't know about that," he said. "Each of the cannons was named for a past king, a tradition passed down from the time of Captain Smith. The two that face the forest in the southeast bulwark are known as Edward Longshanks and John."

"I see." Sam tried to feign interest, but it was rather early and his brain was foggy.

Unconcerned by his brother's lack of interest, William stretched, then grabbed a bit of leftover bread from the previous evening's meal. "Well, I'm off," he said, not seeming the least bit tired after his long night. "Think I'll pay a visit to the Martins before work."

When his brother turned away, Sam grimaced. This was becoming an all too common practice. Instead of taking every opportunity to catch up on sleep, William seemed to be spending more and more of his free time at Mr. Martin's plantation. In fact, he was hanging about so much that it was getting quite hard for Sam to find a private moment to discuss the treasure with Liz.

Luckily, he was able to catch her one morning shortly thereafter. She was out alone tending to the chickens. "Good morning," Sam said tentatively. "I have been hoping to talk with you."

Liz glanced up. "Oh, hello, Sam," she said, giving him only a quick smile. "What is it?"

"It's about the clue." Sam gently kicked away a hen that was pecking hungrily at his shoe. "I was thinking—perhaps we should meet with Matachanna again to see if she knows of anything else it might mean. I have heard that Captain Newport once presented Powhatan with a crown to show respect and good will; perhaps that's what the clue is about."

Liz shrugged, bending down to retrieve a stray egg. "Perhaps," she said. "But I haven't seen Matachanna since we went to the village. I expect she's staying close to home to avoid trouble."

Sam bit his lip. Was it his imagination, or did she not seem particularly interested in the quest anymore? What had changed?

William, he thought. *That's what has changed.*

"All right," he said. "It was just a thought, anyway. I'd better get inside now and see what your father wants me to do today."

He was still feeling vexed by the encounter as he sorted through some old maps and other drawings in Mr. Martin's office later that morning. Thoughts of the way he'd felt with Liz's arms around him were intertwined in his mind with the memory of his brother confidently planning to make her his wife. And now that William's plan seemed already to be underway, how could Sam hope to compete? With his silly little treasure quest that seemed to be going nowhere? That seemed an unlikely form of courtship.

For a moment, he wondered if Hal was right after all. Perhaps it *did* make sense to join forces with Jasper if he ever hoped to make sense of those clues. . . .

As that thought lingered in his mind, he found himself staring down at a crudely-drawn parchment map. He blinked, recognizing it, by the shape of the river, as an area upstream from the settlement. The map consisted mostly of drawings of trees, bodies of water, and a few other features, including what appeared to be a funny little hill shaped just like one of his father's favorite clock casings. . . .

Sam's heart skipped a beat. He started digging frantically through the other maps, not caring that he was destroying his entire morning's work of sorting and organizing. Finally he found another map of the same area and spread it out on the desk. Then he pulled out his notebook.

He broke into a grin as he compared his own sketch of the arrow pattern on the headdress to the shape of that hill on the map. They were a perfect match!

Sixteen

"Are you certain about this?" Liz asked.

It was just before dawn the next morning, and Sam and Liz were in the deserted square between the church and the governor's house. Sam had arranged to meet her at her father's farm, but after hearing his news, she had been too eager to wait and had surprised him by being there outside his barracks when he emerged. Even though he disliked the thought of her crossing the fields alone at that hour, when many wild beasts might be lurking about, his heart had soared to see her there. Clearly, she hadn't lost interest in this mission after all.

"As certain as I can be," Sam said. "If we can find that hillock, we'll find the treasure! I feel it in my bones!"

They hurried toward the back gate of the fort. "Wait here a moment," Sam said, glancing to one side. "I shall just go borrow some digging tools from William's blacksmith shop. We may need them."

"All right. But hurry. We want to be away before anyone awakens and sees us." Liz glanced anxiously at the nearby houses, then hid herself in the small space between two of them, to stay out of sight.

Sam left her and turned down a narrow alley between two buildings nearby, hurrying past several more houses, as well as the tavern and the cooper's little workshop. Soon he'd reached the forge, where he selected a spade and a pick, before heading back to where he'd left Liz. He and Liz had started early, even for this community of farmers. But Sam discovered that everyone else wasn't sleeping at that hour when a man stumbled drunkenly out of the tavern just as he passed. Sam immediately recognized Jasper.

"Gates!" Jasper bellowed, spotting him at the same moment. "Wait there—I wish to speak with you, boy!"

Sam clutched his tools and silently cursed his own bad luck. He was certain that he and Liz could easily outrun Jasper in his current condition, if necessary; he only hoped Jasper didn't have a weapon on him that might change those odds.

"Excuse me," he told Jasper, ducking around him. "I'm in a hurry."

Jasper staggered after him. "Gates!" he slurred irritably.

Sam was glancing back at him, fearing Jasper's shouts would awaken the entire colony, when he felt a strong hand grab his arm. With a gasp, he turned and found himself face to face with Francis Q. Morehead.

"You, boy!" the gentleman said sternly. "What are you doing out here at this hour?"

"N-nothing, sir," Sam stammered. "I was just fetching these tools for my master."

Morehead looked him over with suspicion in his close-set eyes. "Hmmph," he said. "That's as may be. Perhaps you had better come inside so I can ask you a few more questions." He gestured at the tavern.

Sam was all too aware of the sky lightening overhead. If he went with Morehead now, his quest might be delayed another full day or more.

"I'd be happy to," he said. With one quick twist of his arm, he broke free of the man's grip. "Later. As I said, I'm in a hurry at the moment. So sorry, sir!"

He raced off down the alley, ignoring the shouts from both Morehead and the drunken Jasper behind him. Liz was waiting just around the corner, wide-eyed.

"What was all that about?" she panted, grabbing the

pick out of his hand as they both ran for the gate.

"Never mind," Sam replied, giving the sentries a quick wave as they dashed outside. "It's over now."

He was still feeling jittery as they crossed the tributary and entered the forest on the other side. Was his encounter with Jasper a sign of bad luck for this mission? And what had Morehead been doing out and about at that early hour?

An hour later, Sam had all but forgotten about that. The sun was up in earnest now, its strong rays heating the moist air of the forest into a sticky, unpleasant soup. Sweat was pouring down Sam's brow, stinging his eyes and attracting innumerable buzzing insects. The landscape was thickly wooded and also quite rocky, making the going difficult. Sam and Liz often had to thread their way through dense underbrush or climb over extensive outcroppings.

"I wish Matachanna were here," Liz said, waving a hand before her face to shoo away a fly as she crested yet another rocky rise. "She knows this forest better than either of us ever could."

Sam had been entertaining similar thoughts. They had neither guide nor compass, only the simple map, which he'd copied carefully into his notebook. What if they got lost and couldn't find their way back to Jamestown? Once again he wondered at his own wisdom in bringing Liz along on such a risky mission. . . .

"Look!" Her excited shout broke into his thoughts. "There it is!"

Sam glanced forward and saw a tall, craggy outcropping rising above the treetops ahead, like a giant crooked arrow pointing at the sky. He gasped. It was the spitting image of that pattern on the headdress!

"That's it!" he shouted gleefully. "We've found it!"

Heat, insects, and tired feet all forgotten, he and Liz rushed forward. Soon, they'd reached the base of the out-cropping. It sat in a small clearing free of trees, and Sam immediately swung the pick into action, chipping at the hard, dry ground and ignoring the small pain in his shoulder.

Liz joined him, setting to work with the spade. "Oh, dear," she gasped after a moment. "Now I see why laborers have such strong muscles! Digging is hard work!"

Sam glanced at her, suddenly very aware of his own slim build. Was she wishing his brother were there instead, with his stronger back and arms?

Side by side, he and Liz attacked the rocky ground with

a vengeance, awaiting the clink of a metal tool hitting some buried metal-bound trunk. . . .

An hour later they were still digging. The midmorning sun beat down on them mercilessly. Feeling a bit dizzy with heat and exertion, Sam paused to lean upon the handle of his tool.

"This is a fool's mission," he exclaimed. "We could dig for a fortnight and still not cover half of the perimeter of this hillock! Besides, what if the treasure is hidden in the forest nearby, or even up among the rocks somewhere?" He waved a hand up at the arrow-shaped outcropping. "We need more direction."

Liz stopped digging, too. She looked hot and tired; her long, blond hair had escaped from its braid and was clinging to her face, and her skirts were bedraggled.

"Perhaps you're right," she agreed breathlessly, wiping a strand of hair out of her eyes. "But what else can we do but try, now that we're here?"

Part of Sam wanted to agree with her, to keep digging. But the wiser part protested. It was his day off work, but Liz would have been missed by now. The longer they stayed, the more difficulty she would have explaining where she'd been.

"I don't know," he said. "But I think we had better head back. Perhaps we've missed some additional clue somewhere."

By the time he finished his supper that evening, Sam's muscles were protesting from the unaccustomed exertion, and he wanted nothing more than to sleep. But his mind was racing so much that sleep was out of the question.

William was out doing sentry duty again, so Sam pulled out his notebook. For the next hour, he spent precious candle wax poring over it, trying to figure out what he could possibly have missed in Gilbert's clues. How did Gilbert expect anyone to find the treasure with only that outcropping as a clue?

Finally, his mind was nearly as exhausted as his body. He was about to snuff out the candle and go to bed when a faint shadow fell across the notebook page, which was open to the drawing of the map. It was only a spider spinning its way down from the rafters, but Sam stared at it, his mind clicking back into full gear. Then he smiled.

A few minutes later he was racing across the fields outside the fort at full speed. The moon hadn't risen yet, and it was almost pitch black. Several times he nearly fell, but he didn't dare slow his pace.

Liz awoke with a squeak of fright when he touched her on the arm. "What are you doing here?" she cried softly, pulling her bedsheets up to cover her shift and glancing over at her soundly sleeping younger sisters.

"No time to explain," he whispered. "Get dressed as quickly as you can and meet me outside. We have to get back to that arrow place—right now!"

Seventeen

The moon was still low as Sam and Liz raced through the forest. "What's this all about?" Liz cried breathlessly. "I must be deranged to follow you out here in the middle of the night!"

"No time to explain," Sam panted, catching her with his free hand as she tripped over an exposed root. In his other hand, he held the spade and pick, which he'd grabbed once again from the forge. "We have to hurry!"

"Can't we at least wait until the moon comes up?" Liz exclaimed. "The full moon was only days ago—it will still give us plenty of light to see by . . ."

"Hurry!" Sam exclaimed, dragging her along as he ran even faster. "We have to hurry!"

If the earlier trip through the forest had been difficult with the heat and the bugs, it was even more so in the dark. Sam had to rely on his excellent memory to guide them, and even so, he wasn't entirely certain they hadn't gone off track a few times. Once again, he found himself doubting his own wisdom. It was bad enough attempting this himself, let alone bringing Liz along. And what if his wild hunch turned out to be wrong? Most probably Liz would never trust him again, and rightly so. That is, if they didn't end up lost or worse—attacked by wild animals.

But there was no turning back now. "Here we go," Sam cried out, hearing the gurgle of water nearby. "This must be that creek we crossed this morning. Only a little farther now, and we—"

"Oof!" Just then, Liz tripped again. This time she didn't manage to catch herself and went down hard on her stomach with a pained cry.

"Liz!" Sam cried, skidding to a stop. "Are you all right?"

She was already pushing herself to her feet. "I'm fine," she wheezed, leaning against the broad trunk of a tree. "Just irritated my burns a bit, that's all. A moment, please, while I catch my breath . . ."

Sam waited anxiously, peering at her by the faint light of the stars. In the brief moment of quiet, there was a loud *crack* from somewhere nearby, so loud that it briefly silenced the humming nighttime frogs and insects.

"What was that?" Liz hissed, her eyes going wide.

Sam's stomach churned with fear as he stared around, willing his eyes to see in the dark like a cat's. But it was no use. Everything more than an arm's length away in every direction was a shadowy blackness where almost anything could be hiding. Had that noise been made by some fierce animal stalking them? Or perhaps by a native warrior doing the same? It might even be Jasper—what if he'd sobered up enough to somehow follow them out here? Sam wasn't sure which of those three possibilities was the worst.

Still, he was responsible for them being in this position, and he was determined to take the brunt of it in any case. "Hide back there," he whispered, pushing Liz around to the other side of the tree trunk. "Don't make a sound!"

"But—" she protested, her voice shaking.

"Hush!" he hissed as he heard another, crack from somewhere just a few paces away in the dark. Without pausing to think about what he was doing, he threw himself directly at the spot with a wild howl.

Thud! He connected with a something—some*one*—and they both crashed to the hard ground.

"Ow!" A voice—a very familiar voice—cried out.

Sam sat up. "Hal?" he said uncertainly.

There was a flash of light, and a moment later a small torch flared into life to reveal Hal's cranky, moon-shaped face. "What's wrong with you?" he complained. "I hit my shoulder on a rock!"

"What's wrong with *me*?" Sam demanded. "That's rich, coming from the likes of you." Pushing himself to his feet, Sam didn't bother to mention that his own shoulder still ached from where an *arrow* had hit him—but it was tempting.

As Sam glared at Hal, Liz came out from behind the tree. "What are *you* doing here?" she demanded, hands on hips.

Hal held up his torch and peered at her. "I was about to ask you two the same thing."

Sam crossed his arms over his chest, furious at Hal for putting such a fright into them—and now even more for delaying their mission. "It is no business of yours," he said. "You have to turn back. Now."

"No," Hal said stubbornly. "Not until you tell me what's going on."

Sam blew out a breath of frustration. Why did Hal have to be such an infernal bother? He could try to convince him to go back, but he knew that it was no use. Hal wanted to know what they were doing and he wasn't going to be put off. And there was no more time to waste.

"Fine," Sam finally snapped. "Come along, then. But you'll have to keep up—we won't wait for you."

They moved on, faster than ever. Sam ignored the sound of Hal's labored panting, peering forward in search of landmarks. It was getting easier to see them; a faint glow was turning the forest from black to a mealy gray. The moon was rising! That gave Sam an extra spurt of energy, and he sprinted on, soon leaving the complaining Hal well behind.

Liz kept pace with Sam. "Are you ever going to tell me why we're out here?" she said between gasps.

"Soon." Sam spotted the tip of the outcropping over the treetops ahead. It would take too long to walk through the thick, rock-studded woods—he had to find another way to see the spot. He grabbed the trunk of the tallest tree in the vicinity and shimmied up, ignoring the rough bark ripping at his skin.

"Wait for me!" Liz called. When he glanced down he saw her clambering up behind him. Sam couldn't help but smile. Liz was full of surprises.

With effort, they finally pulled themselves above the tree line. From there Sam could see the arrow-shaped out-cropping clearly. He also saw the almost-full moon rising immediately behind it, making the arrow appear to bisect the round disc of the moon.

Just like the design on that headdress, Sam thought, with a smile.

Liz gasped, noticing the same thing. "Look!" she cried, clinging to a branch with one arm and pointing with the other at the long, narrow shadow cast by the outcropping. "The moon is pointing the way!" She glanced up at Sam. "That's why you were in such a hurry, isn't it? You knew that would happen?"

"Yes," Sam said, relieved that his hunch had turned out to be correct—so far, at least. "I was afraid if we missed it tonight, we'd have to wait for the next full moon before we could try again."

They both stared at the shadow for as long as it lasted, trying to memorize the spot in the forest where the shadowy tip of the arrow was pointing. Luckily, there were several other distinctive outcroppings and chunks of rock in that direction, as well as a creek gleaming in the moonlight, so

Sam felt confident that they'd be able to find it even from the ground.

Finally, the moon rose free of the outcropping, pouring its pale light across the forest unencumbered. Sam and Liz shimmied down the tree to find Hal waiting for them. "Well?" he demanded petulantly. "What was that all about? Liz, Mother is going to have a fit when she sees the state your skirt is in."

Liz laughed. "Not when she sees the treasure I've brought home!"

As they made their way through the moonlit forest toward the spot the shadow arrow had indicated, they explained the whole thing to Hal. Sam had all but forgiven the other boy, now that the first part of the trip had been successful. But that didn't stop him from making Hal take a nice, long turn at the shovel once they'd reached the right spot, a grassy clearing near the creek.

Before long, they had each taken two turns digging, without discovering a thing. Sam was starting to fear that he'd been mistaken yet again. Could there be something else that he'd missed?

With a frustrated groan, he shoved the spade into the

soft dirt near the creek, driving it in with his foot. But it stopped short with a *thunk*.

"What was that?" Liz heard the noise and ran over immediately.

Hal grunted from where he lay exhausted on the grass. "Prob'ly just another rock," he mumbled.

But Sam yanked the spade loose, then carefully began scooping out the dirt in that spot. Once he'd cleared the top layer Liz helped, using her hands to pull away the loose dirt beneath. Within minutes they'd unearthed a metal box about the size of a large book.

By now Hal had come over to watch. "Open it!" he said eagerly. "Is it the treasure? It's rather small, isn't it?"

The box was held shut by a rusty metal lock. Sam easily knocked it loose with the spade, then kneeled down to open the lid. All three let out gasps.

There, lying on a bed of aged velvet, three large golden coins gleamed in the moonlight.

Eighteen

"We did it!" Sam shouted in exultation, leaping to his feet and punching the air gleefully. "We found it! We found the treasure!"

"You mean *you* did it!" Liz cried with a smile. "I was ready to give up, but you figured it out!" She got up and danced around the clearing with him, holding her skirt in both hands.

"This is it?" Hal was still on his knees staring into the box. He grabbed one of the coins and held it up. "Three lousy coins?"

Sam stopped dancing and glared at him. "That's three more coins than *you* would have found on your own, you ungrateful wretch."

He snatched the coin from Hal and examined it. It was a little larger than a common Venetian ducat and more roughly made. The only design etched on its face was what appeared to be an oddly-shaped letter Y. Could it be

Spanish, perhaps left by earlier explorers and unearthed by the Roanoke settlers or by Gilbert himself?

Liz picked up another of the coins and turned it over in her hands. "These look old, and quite special, really. They may be worth something."

"True enough. And at least there are three of them," Hal said. "That means one for each of us." He grabbed the last coin.

Sam glared at him. He hadn't been thinking of how to divide the spoils yet. It hardly seemed fair that Hal should get a full third, especially when Sam himself had done almost all the work. He didn't mind sharing with Liz, of course, but would have preferred that the third coin go to William or perhaps Matachanna if she had any desire for it.

But Hal had already slipped the coin into his clothes. Sam realized that, short of beating him with the spade (which was quite tempting), he wasn't likely to get it back.

In any case, it's not as if one gold coin shall make any of us rich beyond imagining, he thought. *Perhaps it's better that Elias didn't live to this moment—he might have been sorely disappointed with where the hunt led.*

Sam had to admit to a twinge of disappointment himself. Why all the clues and bother to hide such a paltry treasure? Had there once been more, perhaps, previously found by others? He supposed he would never know.

Nevertheless, it was exciting just to figure out the puzzle, Sam reminded himself. *Even if it didn't lead to any fabled Treasure of the Ancients.* He shot a look at Liz. *Besides, if not for the treasure hunt, I might never have had the opportunity to spend so much time with Liz. And that has been a treasure of a different kind in itself. . . .*

He returned his attention to the coin in his hand, and the strange marking on its face. Perhaps . . . but no. He smiled at the nagging feeling telling him that, once again, he might be missing something. How could he entertain such thoughts with actual gold right here in his hand? No, it was time to ignore such feelings and simply enjoy his triumph.

The following day, Sam walked to the Martin farm as if nothing had happened. He had arrived home from his adventure to find that William was still on sentry duty, and so he hadn't yet had a chance to tell his brother about the coin now hidden in his right shoe, its round, hard shape pressing into his foot with each step across the fields.

The feel of the gold reminded him that he still wasn't

sure what he would do with his treasure. The practical part of his nature told him to take whatever someone would give him for it in goods, whether food or other necessities. But that seemed an unworthy fate for something that had cost him so much thought and effort. Besides, he still hadn't quite shaken the feeling from the night before. It might be foolish, but he knew that until he settled that in his mind, he wouldn't feel right letting the coin out of his possession.

By the time he headed back across the fields that evening, his right foot was sore from stepping on the coin all day, and he was chiding himself for hiding it there. Mr. Martin had sent him out on errands to the fort several times, plus he'd been asked to help catch the Martins' ornery horse, Venture. The animal had broken loose while Liz was away and galloped through the fields trampling the crops. After all that, Sam found himself limping slightly as he entered the fort and headed for home.

Still, by the next morning the ache in his foot had faded more than his desire not to let his treasure leave his person. As he got dressed, he tucked the coin into his left shoe instead of his right, hoping he could avoid so much running around that day. When he arrived at the Martins' homestead a short while later, he found Liz waiting for him at the water trough. She looked nervous.

"What's the matter?" he asked.

"It's that man, Jasper," she said. "He cornered me last evening while I was out checking on Venture. He threatened to hurt me if I didn't tell him where you keep the treasure map." She shook her head. "My father came out to see what was delaying me and chased him off, but I have a feeling he'll be back."

"Did you tell him about the coins?" Sam asked. When she shook her head, he sighed. It was one thing for Jasper to bother him; it was another thing completely to harass Liz.

Checking anxiously for anyone who might be nearby, Liz led him away from the house to a private spot behind a grove of trees. "What shall we do?" she asked. "I fear he'll keep after us until he gets what he wants."

Sam opened his mouth to answer, but another man's words came before he could speak. "You're right about that, young lady," Jasper hissed, stepping out of the trees and grabbing Liz by the throat before either she or Sam could react.

"Jasper!" Sam blurted out. "Let her go! It's me you want."

"Yes," Jasper said, tightening his grip on Liz's throat. "But you keep slipping away. Perhaps if I strangle your lady friend, it might loosen your tongue a bit."

Sam held up both hands. "All right, stop!" he cried. "I'll tell you the truth. That was no map I got from Elias; it was a letter. We followed its clues, and—"

"Never mind that, boy," Jasper interrupted. "I want you to tell me where I can find the gold coins that you found."

Sam's heart sank. Hal must have betrayed them. His shoulders slumped, and he shuffled his left foot, feeling the familiar press of the coin.

"All right, I'll tell you," he said wearily. A few bits of gold weren't worth Liz's life.

"That's more like it." Jasper smiled grimly, loosening his grip on Liz's neck.

Before Sam could go on, a rock flew out of the nearby trees and struck Jasper on the temple. The older man let go of Liz and grabbed his head with both hands.

"I've been shot!" he cried out in a panicky voice.

"Come on!" Seeing his chance, Sam grabbed Liz by the hand and ran toward the house.

Soon they were safely within view of several of the

Martins' field workers, as well as Mr. Martin himself, who was surveying his fields from atop Venture's saddle. The man gave them a quizzical look before returning his gaze to the fields. Clearly, his daughter's odd behavior was nothing new to him.

"Whew!" Sam said, glancing behind to make sure Jasper hadn't followed them into the open. "That was close. Where did that rock come from, I wonder?"

"It was Matachanna." Liz's voice was shaky, and she was touching her throat gingerly with her fingertips. "I caught a glimpse of her running away. She must have been looking for me and saw what was happening."

"Thank the Lord that she did," Sam declared. "I can't believe Jasper was willing to strangle you over three gold coins!" He paused, that nagging feeling returning stronger than ever. "Or was he?"

"What do you mean?"

Instead of answering, Sam kicked off his left shoe and fished out his coin. He stared at the crooked *Y* on it thoughtfully.

"The coins aren't the treasure," he said slowly, his brain going into high gear. "They're just another clue!"

Liz let out a loud gasp. "Are you sure?"

"No," Sam admitted. "But it must be so. It's the only thing that makes sense! Hal must have told Jasper about the coins, and Jasper has figured out the same thing—that's why he's so greedy for the coins. He must know the "map" he's been searching for doesn't exist. So he wants to figure out the next clue himself!"

"Wait here." Liz raced for the house, returning moments later clutching her own coin. "Here," she panted, shoving it into Sam's hand. "Mine has a funny sort of Z on it."

Sam looked at the zigzag etching on the second coin. "Y, Z," he said. "That doesn't seem to have much meaning. But maybe Hal's coin will tie it together somehow. . . ."

They found Liz's brother cooling his feet in the river with a fishing pole abandoned nearby. But when they told him they needed to see his coin, he shrugged.

"I don't have it anymore," he said. "I sold it to Jasper."

"What?" Sam and Liz cried at once.

Liz immediately started scolding her brother for his greed. Sam didn't bother to join in. He'd already guessed that Jasper had learned about the coins from Hal; it was not a surprise that Hal had stooped to such a level. Now Sam's mind was clicking along, looking for a way around this latest problem.

"Never mind," he said, speaking more to himself than to the others. "If Jasper has that coin now, there's only one solution."

"Work with him?" Hal asked hopefully. "That's what I've been saying all along!"

"No." Sam turned to stare at the fort in the distance. "We steal that coin back!"

Nineteen

The next morning, Sam huddled around the corner from Jasper's lodgings with Liz and Hal beside him.

"Everyone ready?" he asked briskly.

Liz nodded. "We'll stand guard at either end of the place and give Matachanna's whistle if anyone comes," she promised.

Hal rolled his eyes. "I still think this is a foolish plan," he complained. But at the dark looks from the other two, he added, "Don't worry, I'll do it."

They waited in hiding until they saw Jasper emerge from the place and head off down the street toward the well site. Then Sam sneaked into the building and quickly found Jasper's room, which was modest and nearly bare. It didn't take long to search the treasure hunter's meager store of possessions. There was no sign of the coin.

"He must have it on him," Sam reported, once he'd rejoined the others outside. "Time for plan two."

That evening, Sam met Hal and Liz in an increasingly familiar spot—around the corner from the colony's tavern. "Did you get it?" he asked Liz as soon as the three were together.

Liz nodded. "Matachanna said only to use a little," she said, pulling out a small packet and handing it over. "It has a strong, bitter taste."

"So does Father's whiskey," Hal said with a snort as he held up the bottle he was carrying. "Give it here."

"I'll do it." Sam grabbed the bottle and dumped in a bit of the powder from the packet. He hesitated, wondering if it would be enough. He certainly didn't want to overdo it and kill him. . . .

"Hurry!" Liz whispered. "He's coming."

Jasper was walking toward the tavern, whistling. "Go on," Sam hissed, quickly capping the bottle, shoving it into Hal's arms, and giving him a push. "Do not fail us!"

Hal stumbled out right into Jasper's path. "H-hello!" Hal said, his voice sounding overly loud and nervous to Sam's ear.

Luckily, Jasper seemed not to notice. "Ah, there's my young business partner," he said jovially. "Haven't changed your mind about that gold coin, have you?"

"On the contrary." Hal held up the bottle. "I was hoping we could have a drink together in celebration of our recent arrangement. I even swiped my father's best whiskey."

Jasper licked his lips. "Whiskey, eh?" he said. "Can't say no to that, can I? Come inside, boy, and let's drink!"

"Er—inside?" Hal hesitated.

Sam and Liz exchanged a glance. Would he be able to pull this off?

"What if he goes in and somebody else helps himself to that whiskey?" Liz whispered.

She needn't have worried. Hal spoke up, suggesting they drink it somewhere more private—"so as to have it all for ourselves," he finished.

Jasper laughed heartily. "A man after my own heart!" he exclaimed, slinging an arm around Hal's shoulders. "Very well, then. Let's find a spot where Reverend Whitaker isn't likely to come along and interrupt us with lectures about temperance."

Soon the pair were seated on a pair of barrels behind the tavern drinking the whiskey out of the pewter cups Hal had brought. At least Jasper was drinking—Sam could see Hal surreptitiously pouring out his cup every time the older man looked away. Jasper made a few initial complaints about the bitter taste of the whiskey, but it didn't stop him from drinking down three servings. Within minutes, he was passed out on the ground, snoring loudly.

"It worked!" Liz exclaimed. She and Sam had followed the drinkers and were spying from nearby.

Hal heard her and hurried over. "What now?" he hissed.

"Get the coin back," Sam told him quietly but urgently. "Search his clothes!"

Hal wrung his hands, glancing back at the unconscious man. "Why should I have to do it?" he cried. "I've done enough for this stupid plan already!" Pausing just long enough to grab the whiskey bottle, he raced off.

"Hal!" Liz called after him, sounding furious. But he was already gone. "What a coward," she said. "Shall I go after him?"

"Never mind." Sam stepped forward, wondering just how long Matachanna's potion would keep Jasper sleeping. "I'll do it."

He stepped forward, taking a deep breath as he looked down at Jasper's lean face, sinister even in sleep. Then he crouched over and began rifling through the man's clothes. Liz crept forward and watched over his shoulder.

"Got it!" Sam whispered, his fingers closing over a familiar round shape tucked into Jasper's belt.

At that moment the man groaned and stirred. His eyes fluttered and started to open. Sam stared down at him, transfixed, the coin grasped in one hand.

"Move," Liz hissed, shoving him hard. By the time Jasper's eyes opened fully and focused, it was her smiling face that hovered above him. "Ah, there we are," she said in a loud, cheerful voice. "Thought we were going to be off to the burial grounds with you after that fall!"

"What?" Jasper coughed and struggled to sit up. "Where am I? What happened?"

Liz firmly pushed him back down onto the ground. "Now, now," she chided gently. "Stay still, don't overtax yourself so soon. You tripped and fell down, don't you recall? Here, let me help soothe that bump on your head." She ripped a bit of cloth off the hem of her shift and dipped it in a puddle that smelled suspiciously of dog urine. Then she slapped it across Jasper's forehead, covering his eyes. "There, that's better. . . ."

She jumped to her feet quick as a wink. Sam had been lurking just out of Jasper's sight and followed as she raced around the corner. They both burst into quiet laughter when they heard Jasper's outraged roar behind them.

"Quick—this way." Sam pulled her around the corner. They both nearly ran into Francis Q. Morehead, who was striding down the street toward the tavern. "Oh! Begging your pardon, sir," Sam mumbled, preparing to hurry on past him.

But Morehead stopped him with a grip on his arm. "Hang on, Gates," he said sternly. "I wish to speak with you about a certain coin I've heard is in your possession."

Sam gasped. How did Morehead know about the coins?

Jasper! he thought, suddenly remembering Hal's comment about seeing Morehead and Jasper drinking together in the tavern. And then there was the time Morehead had appeared early in the morning—when Jasper was around. Sam's heart thudded in his chest. *They must be cohorts!*

Mumbling an excuse about Liz and her father being angry, Sam wrenched his arm free, grabbed Liz's hand, and ran.

They lost Morehead easily in the maze of buildings

within the fort. Soon they were sitting on a fallen log in a field some distance outside, watching the rosy glow of the setting sun turn the river into a rainbow.

"That was close!" Sam exclaimed. "Good thing Morehead didn't know we have the third coin back, or he mightn't have let us go so easily."

"Indeed." Liz glanced back at the fort, a worried crease marking her brow. "But he'll know it once Jasper finds him. We shall have to be careful—and figure this out quickly."

Sam nodded. "Do you have your coin?"

"Yes. Here it is." Liz pulled it out and handed it to him.

Sam laid the three coins side by side on the rough bark of the log. He and Liz crouched on their heels and stared at them.

"Yours has a *Y*," Liz said, tracing it with her finger. "A funny sort of *Y*, a bit off-kilter. Oh—and see? There's a dot in the crook of it."

Sam looked closer. She was right—a tiny dot was nestled in the V-shaped part on the top. "I wonder if that means something, or if it's just an imperfection in the gold." He shifted his gaze to the next coin. "Yours has the zigzag *Z*," he said. "And now we have Hal's . . ."

Liz leaned closer, her pale hair falling against the log as she peered at the third coin. "Why, his is the oddest of all," she said. "The etching looks like a lowercase *T*, and beside it, an arrow with four feathers or notches on the shaft."

Sam picked up the third coin and studied it. What did it mean? He had to admit he had no idea. "If this is supposed to spell out some kind of clue, I must say I can't work it out," he said with a sigh. Still, he pulled out his notebook and set each coin beneath a page to make a rubbing of the patterns. Then he and Liz hid the coins beneath a rock near the water. There was nothing more to be done until something came to one of them. Fighting back his frustration, Sam bid Liz good night and the two parted ways.

That evening Sam sat up for an hour studying the rubbings, trying to make sense of the markings on the coins. Finally he gave up and went to bed, but his dreams were haunted by tumbling, crooked letters throughout much of the night.

In the morning he snuck out of the fort early to avoid any chance of encountering Jasper or Morehead. When he reached the plantation, Hal was waiting for him at Liz's usual spot by one of the water troughs.

"There you are," Hal said, hurrying forward with a frown. "I thought I'd have to wait about all day for you!"

"What do you mean? And where is Liz."

"Never mind." Hal was already hurrying off toward the tributary. "Come along."

"Where are we going?" Sam caught up easily with Hal's slow, rolling stride.

Hal glanced over at him. "Liz is meeting with that pet savage of hers." He wrinkled his nose. "She's an odd one, she is, that funny-looking native girl. In any case, Liz wanted me to bring you."

They found Liz and Matachanna perched on the log examining the coins. Looking up to greet Sam, Liz's eyes twinkled with excitement.

"Matachanna thinks she has the answer!" she cried.

Twenty

"What is it?" Sam asked eagerly. "Matachanna, what can the coins mean?"

The native girl glanced up at him shyly, pushing back her long, black hair. "I am not certain of these two," she said in her soft voice, indicating the *Z* and *T* coins. "But I recognize this one." She held up the *Y* coin. "It shows the . . ." She added one more word, a long, complicated-sounding one, in her native tongue.

"That's a river near here," Liz supplied helpfully. She was practically bouncing up and down with excitement. "Matachanna thinks the coin is a map! The dot tells us to go to the spot where the river branches out."

Suddenly, it all made sense to Sam. What they'd assumed were meant to be letters weren't letters at all; they were merely more maps. Why hadn't he seen it earlier? He could almost hear his father's disapproval. "We should go now," Sam said eagerly. "Who knows when Jasper will find us again? Matachanna, can you take us to this spot?"

"Yes," she said. "We can go now."

At first Hal was reluctant to set off on another trek through the woods. But when Liz pointed out that it was easier than a day's work on the farm, he quickly agreed. She ran back to the house just long enough to tell her father that Sam had stayed in bed with a fever and that she and Hal were off to help a neighbor find a lost calf. She also took the opportunity to grab a few tools from the shed. Then she rejoined the others, and they all set off through the woods.

Having Matachanna lead the way made this trip much easier than the last. She knew the quickest route through the trees, across the creeks and rivers, and around the difficult rocky areas. As they walked, she pointed out which fruits and berries were safe to eat. For the second time that day, Sam found himself thinking of home. He couldn't help but wonder at how different his new life was turning out to be. Back in England, he would never have spent so much time out of doors, and there was certainly no wild vegetation to eat. Everything and everyone was so staid and structured. Sam couldn't help but smile. While life was by no means easy here, he found it far more agreeable.

Before long they were fording a broad but shallow river to reach the V-shaped area where it split in two around a rise in the land. "Look!" Liz cried, pointing. "The crooked Z!"

Her sharp eyes had spotted a large tree that had been split in half and partially charred by lightning. "Of course!" Sam said. "It wasn't a Z at all, but a bolt of lightning meant to point us to this tree." He shook his head and smiled. That Gilbert had been clever indeed! "I wonder if he had these coins made himself, perhaps with help from the natives," he mused. "Or did he use something that he found, just like that verse on board the ship?"

"Who cares?" Hal plunged forward eagerly. "Come, let's dig!"

"Wait," Sam said. "What about the third coin?" He pulled it out and looked at it.

Hal shrugged impatiently, pushing his pale hair off his sweaty, broad forehead. "What about it?" he said. "The other coins led us here, right? Surely the treasure's buried beneath this tree."

"No, Sam's right," Liz said. "The last coin must provide an additional clue." She peered at it in Sam's hand. "Could the four notches on the arrow mean the treasure is four paces from the tree?"

"I was just thinking the same thing," Sam said, impressed as always by her quick mind. "But four paces in which direction?"

"Who cares?" Hal said again. "Just start digging. We're sure to find it eventually."

Sam shook his head. "That could take days," he pointed out, kicking at a small cluster of stones that went bouncing off toward the water's edge. "This rocky soil will not be easy for digging." He looked at Matachanna. "This little *T* must indicate the direction somehow. What are the landmarks near here? Are there any that begin with a *T*, either in our language or yours?"

Matachanna turned slowly around, looking thoughtful. "Our village is that way," she said, pointing. "Over there is the mouth of the big river, and the sea lies out there. . . ." She went on, naming several more landmarks. But none of them began with *T* in either language.

"Are we certain it's meant to be a *T*?" Liz peered at the coin again. "After all, we thought a river was a *Y* and a lightning bolt a *Z* . . . ."

"That's it!" Sam cried. "Liz, you're a genius!"

"I am?" She smiled, looking confused. "I am glad to hear it. But what did I say to help?"

Sam smiled back. "What you just said reminded me that there's one more landmark Matachanna left out," he said. "Jamestown."

Hal wrinkled his nose. "What—you mean because *town* starts with a *T*? Seems a bit far-fetched."

"No." Sam held up the coin so they could all see it clearly. "It's not a *T* at all—it's a cross. It indicates we should measure the paces toward the only Christian settlement in this area. And that's Jamestown!"

Liz gasped. "You're right!" she cried. "It makes perfect sense!"

Hal still looked a bit skeptical. But once Matachanna pointed out which way the fort lay, the others paced off four strides in that direction and started digging. Soon even Hal was caught up in their excitement and took his turn with the spade and pick. It wasn't long before the pick struck metal.

"It's here!" Hal shouted, mopping his sweaty brow. "The treasure—we found it!"

They dug out a metal box. "It's rather small, isn't it?" Liz said in surprise. "Even smaller than the one with the coins."

Sam pried open the rusty lid. There was nothing inside but a quantity of black dust.

"Gunpowder," Sam said. He sighed. "It must be another clue."

"Argh!" Hal exclaimed. "Blast that Gilbert! Why couldn't he have just been straightforward?"

Sam stared at the black powder. "He wanted to make sure the treasure wasn't found by anyone unworthy of it," he said slowly. "He was testing his cousins—or anyone else who might stumble upon it, like us."

Hal scowled. "Well, I'm as worthy as anyone," he grumbled. "I don't care if some old dead scoundrel thinks so."

He continued to complain. But Sam wasn't listening anymore. Gunpowder. What could that mean?

"The next clue might lie with a musket," he mused aloud. "But how would he know that a musket would stay in the colony? No, it must be something more permanent." His eyes lit up as the answer came to him. "Something like—"

"A cannon!" Liz finished for him.

"Yes. But which cannon? There are at least a dozen in

the fort, not to mention those on the ships. . . ." Sam closed
the box and examined it more carefully. "Look, there's
something carved on the lid." He brushed off the rust and
dirt as best he could, then peered at it. "It says M. Cart."

"Is that someone's name?" Hal asked, finally looking
interested again. "Is it someone we're supposed to ask for
the real treasure map?"

"I doubt it," Liz said. "Gilbert was too careful for that.
He would know that people could easily die, or betray him
and take the treasure for themselves."

Sam ran his fingers over the etched letters, thinking
hard. Then his hand stopped. "Wait," he said. "I missed a
letter—there's one more at the end. It's too black with rust
to see anymore, but I can feel it."

Liz pushed his hand aside and felt with her own slender
fingers. "I think it's an *A*," she reported. "So—M. Carta."

Sam smiled. "M. Carta—Magna Carta!" he said.
"That's it. I know which cannon we want!"

Twenty-one

"But wait," Hal said, panting as he hurried along at Sam's heels. They were all rushing back through the forest toward the settlement, still led by Matachanna. "If the treasure is buried beneath a cannon at the settlement, there's little chance of us digging it up without others seeing. There are people about all day and sentries on the bulwarks all night lately, thanks to the sav—" He cut himself off, glancing sheepishly toward Matachanna. "Er, thanks to the many dangers of this land," he finished.

Sam didn't slow his pace. "All we can do is go take a look."

Matachanna left them when they neared the settlement, wanting to get home before anyone noticed she was missing. After a hasty good-bye, Sam, Liz, and Hal continued on into the fort. It was nearly midday by then, and the smells of cooking were everywhere as women worked at preparing the early-afternoon meal. There were not many people on the street, but Sam was careful to keep a lookout for Jasper and Morehead.

He led the way to the southeast bulwark. "When are you going to tell us how you knew which cannon was meant?" Liz asked, a bit breathless from the brisk walk.

Sam smiled at her. "In a moment—when I find out if I'm right."

There was only one sentry on duty in the bulwark at that hour, an older man named Henry who was leaning on one of the cannons picking his teeth with a twig. "What is it?" he asked lazily when they climbed up to the raised bulwark.

"Nothing, sir," Sam answered politely. "We were only hoping to take a look around. I am still rather new here, and my friends tell me there is a lovely view of the river from here, and that I really must take a closer look at the most impressive cannons."

The man rolled his eyes and shrugged. "Look away, then," he said in a tone that indicated he thought it a rather foolish errand. Then he returned his attention to picking his teeth.

Sam walked over to the palisade and peered over the top,

pretending to ooh and aah over the view, which really was quite impressive. It was easy to see why the fort had been built in this spot, despite the disadvantages of swampy land, limited space, and lack of fresh water. Any ship coming up the river could be seen well in advance; the Spanish would never be able to surprise them here.

After a moment he turned back. A quick glance at Henry showed that the man was now fully occupied with using the same twig to pry the grime from beneath his fingernails.

Sam walked over to one of the cannons. "Ah, but these are indeed most impressive," he said. "My brother William tells me they are all named after our great kings."

Henry glanced up at him in surprise. "William?" he said. "You're the brother William Gates is always on about? Scrawny thing, ain't ye?" When Sam nodded, the man went on. "Aye, the cannons all carry names." Henry patted the one he was leaning against. "This fellow here is Edward the First. That one over there is Richard the Third. And the one behind you is named for old John Plantagenet."

"I see." Sam shot Liz a meaningful look.

She caught on quickly. "If you please, sir," she said in a

lilting, girlish voice that caused Sam to smile. "I have been wondering about some of the things one can see from here, if perhaps you could advise me . . . ?"

Sam didn't listen as she prattled on, distracting the sentry by pointing out various things on the riverbank and beyond. He stepped over to the cannon named after King John. Perhaps Hal was right, and the treasure was buried in the ground beneath this spot. But then again, perhaps not. Gilbert would have no way of knowing whether this cannon might be moved to a different spot on the bulwark or even elsewhere in the fort entirely. No, unless Sam missed his guess, there had to be another clue on the cannon itself.

It took him only moments to find it. Ducking down to peer beneath the cannon's solid curved barrel, he spotted a crude design carved into the metal. After checking to be sure Liz still had the sentry occupied, he pulled a page from his notebook and quickly made a rubbing, which he tucked away without giving it so much as a glance. There would be time enough for that once they were away.

"All right," he said when he was finished, interrupting Liz's series of questions about the native waterfowl. "I suppose we'd better leave you alone now. Many thanks, sir."

Soon the three of them were hidden among some trees on the riverbank near the Martin homestead. "All right, *now* will you tell us what's going on, Gates?" Hal demanded petulantly. "You're acting most ridiculously mysterious."

"For once, I find myself agreeing with my brother," Liz said with a smile. "What did you find on that cannon, Sam? And how did you know where to look?"

"I shall answer the second question first," Sam said. "The clue was on that box we dug up. The gunpowder, of course, indicated that it was a cannon we wanted—Gilbert had to have known those would be unlikely to leave the colony anytime soon. The words on the lid of the box told us which cannon to check for the next clue."

"You mean M. Carta?" Liz tilted her head. "I know the Magna Carta was the Great Charter of Freedoms that the king was forced to sign back in the thirteenth century. But how—" She gasped, hearing her own words. "Oh, I see! It was King John who signed it. And that particular cannon was named after him by the first settlers!"

Sam grinned, pleased that she'd figured it out at last. "Correct." He held out the rubbing he'd made. "Now let's take a look at what old King John had to tell us."

They huddled over the rubbing. Sam gasped when he got a good look at it—it was a clock face! With a jolt, he remembered all the times he'd seen his father bent over similar numbered faces.

"What is it—a picture of a compass?" Hal asked.

"No, it's a clock." Sam pointed. "See the numbers?"

"But see here." Hal pushed his hand away and pointed to another spot on the rubbing. "That's not a number, it's a letter—the letter *W*, like for 'west' on a compass face."

Liz took the paper and peered at it closely. "He's right. The letter *W* stands where the nine should be. What could it mean? Is this another map—could the *W* be another winding river or some such?"

"I don't know." Sam stared at the paper. "But the *W* does lie just where it would on a compass, so it could be trying to point us west. But west of where? And what does the clock face mean?"

Suddenly, Hal's round face lit up. "I know!" he crowed. "Oh, I can't believe it—I've actually figured it out before you two! How do you like that? Good thing you didn't succeed in cutting me out, eh?" He grinned at them triumphantly.

Sam frowned. "What are you on about?"

"Yes," Liz said. "If you think you know something, then tell us."

Hal was still grinning. "Can't you two see?" he said. "It's terribly obvious. The *W* does stand for West—*Thomas* West, which is the given name of Baron De La Warr. After all, he was the owner of one of the only modern *clocks* in this settlement!"

Sam gasped. "That's it!" he cried, breaking into a giddy smile. "Hal, you must be right! But how did you figure it?"

"I'm not quite so feebleminded as you thought, eh?"

"It's only because of the clock," Liz said, though she was smiling, too. "Hal always takes note of rare, expensive things such as that. When did you catch a glimpse of it, Hal? On our voyage over on the *Deliverance*, or later after we arrived here?"

Suddenly Sam's giddy mood evaporated. "Hold on," he said glumly. "De La Warr returned to England last year! That means this may be a real dead end, one that Gilbert probably didn't anticipate, being that West had been declared governor for life of the colony, and . . ." Suddenly he noticed that while Liz looked equally deflated, Hal was still grinning. "What?"

"West may be gone," Hal said. "But his clock remains in Jamestown. He must have given it to the current governor before he left."

Liz gasped. "How do you know?" she cried.

"I saw it." Hal cast a quick sidelong glance at Sam. "It was sitting upon a shelf in the room where I sneaked in to grab that document case."

Sam nodded, hope flooding back through him. "That's it, then!" he said. "Hal, you've already named our next move."

"I have? What did I say?"

"We must sneak into the governor's house and get a look at that clock!"

Twenty-two

"That's insane!" Hal exclaimed. "We cannot sneak into the governor's home."

"Why not?" Sam replied. "You did it once, did you not?"

"Exactly! And look what came of that!"

"Are you certain of this?" Liz asked Sam worriedly. "Is there no other way?"

"None that will get us the information we need before Jasper and his lot can catch up to us." They had come this far—Sam couldn't stand the thought of being foiled now. "Besides, after sneaking into Chief Powhatan's longhouse, this shall seem like nothing." He forced a laugh, though the memory of that day still sent a shiver through him. "I might be hanged for it, but at least I shan't be tortured along the way."

Suddenly there was a soft whistle from nearby. A moment later, Matachanna stepped out and walked toward them.

Sam felt a twinge of guilt over his comment about being tortured. He hoped Matachanna hadn't heard—he had meant nothing against her people by it.

"What is it, Matachanna?" Liz hurried to meet her. "You look worried."

"It is my father," Matachanna said breathlessly. "He is coming! A group of warriors is with him, and they shall be at your fort within a short time. He says he merely wishes to speak with your leader, but I wanted to warn you, in case . . ." Her voice trailed off, and she shrugged. "Things have not been well between our peoples. I know not what will come of this meeting."

"Thank you, Matachanna." Liz glanced at the others. "Perhaps it would be best if we spent some time in the forest. Just in case."

"No," Sam said. "This could be our chance! The governor and his men will be busy with this delegation. It is just the distraction we need!"

Hal perched gingerly on the edge of Sam's bed, looking around the small room with obvious distaste. "You live *here*?" he said. "Your brother and you both?"

"For the third time, yes," Sam said impatiently. He and Liz were seated at the small, rough table. "Come now, we must hurry," he told her. "The natives will arrive soon, and then I shall have only a little time to sneak in, take a look at the clock, and escape again."

"But that is the problem," Liz argued. "I think I should be the one to sneak in this time."

"But my memory—"

"Yes, your memory is a wonder," she said with a sigh. "But if they catch you, you said it yourself—you shall be hanged. Dale's Code allows nothing less, and sharing the governor's name is unlikely to help you now that doubt has been cast upon your family's honor." She shot a glare toward her brother during that last part.

"Oh, let him go," Hal said, picking curiously at Sam's rough bedsheet. "He seems to be good at this sneaking around."

Sam shot him a glance. It was perhaps the closest thing to a compliment he'd had from Hal.

But Liz was unconvinced. "No," she said firmly. "I shall go this time. If I'm caught, I can pretend I am looking to borrow something from the kitchen. Nobody will think anything of it. It is much safer for all."

Sam hesitated. He had to agree that she had a point. She was female, the daughter of a respected gentleman of the settlement. As she said, she could get away with things he couldn't merely because of who she was.

"Well . . ." he said uncertainly.

"Good!" Liz stood up, smiled, and smoothed her skirt. "Then it is decided. As soon as Powhatan arrives, I shall go. You two can wait here for my return."

At that moment a shout went up from the sentry. "Sounds as if the savages are here," Hal remarked, stepping to the room's small window and peering out. "Better get going then, Liz."

"Right. I'm off." Liz tossed them both one last smile, then slipped out of the room.

Sam touched the wooden planks of the door as it shut behind her. His mind was spinning. Had he just made a mistake by letting her go? How could he be more terrified by the thought of Liz putting herself in danger than he would be were it himself out there? The answer nagged at him, and he quickly pushed it down, focusing on the piece of paper in front of him instead.

The next thirty minutes passed as slowly as any in his life. He and Hal didn't have much to say to each other; they merely sat there, waiting, each with his own thoughts. Finally, just when Sam was about to go out to check on what was happening, the door opened again and Liz slipped back inside, out of breath and with spots of pink in her cheeks.

Sam was too relieved to speak. But Hal stood immediately and stepped toward his sister. "Did you get a look at the clock?"

"I did better than that." Liz reached into her skirts—and pulled out a small, wooden-cased clock with a gold face.

Sam gasped. "You *took* it?" he cried, his tongue loosened at last. "Zounds! But why? You were only supposed to look for the next clue!"

"I know. But look." Liz pointed at the clock's case. It was decorated with an elaborate pattern of scrolling vines and flowers, along with a line of verse beneath the face. "These vines look like they could be a map, and I knew I would never be able to remember it all as you would. And the governor and the others are still talking with Powhatan in the square in front of the church." She shrugged. "You can sketch it in your notebook, and then I'll take it back before

243

anyone has a chance to notice it was ever gone."

Sam bit his lip, feeling anxious. Sneaking into the house was serious enough, but stealing the governor's valuable property? The gallows flashed in Sam's mind, and he shuddered. Still, what was done was done.

"Let's have a look," he said, reaching for his notebook.

He quickly sketched the vines as best he could. Hal watched over his shoulder, his hot breath tickling Sam's neck.

"It *does* look like a map," Hal said after a moment.

Sam had to agree. The larger vines resembled the local rivers, while other parts of the design appeared to indicate additional bits of the landscape. A single small jewel was set into one spot in the pattern. "This is it, then," he said with a shiver. "Perhaps we've finally reached the end of the trail!" He quickly finished the sketch, then jotted down the words beneath the face: *Knowledge is the True Wealth of the Ancients.*

"There's one more mark there." Liz pointed to a small insignia Sam hadn't noticed.

He peered at it and gasped. "Oh," he said slowly. "That's just the clockmaker's mark." He stared at the tiny, familiar insignia: BPG. Benjamin Patrick Gates. This was one of his father's own clocks! Sam wondered at the chance that had carried it from his father's hands to his own. Clearly someone had added the maplike pattern of vines after its arrival in the New World, but indeed, the rest of the clock showed the quality and attention to detail of Benjamin Gates's finest work. Pride surged through him.

"What are you waiting for?" Hal prompted. "Come on, let's return the clock so we can go find the treasure!" He rubbed his pudgy hands together. "How about that line, eh? 'Wealth of the Ancients.' D'you suppose that means the treasure we're after is the Treasure of the Ancients that Jasper's always on about? He says it consists of more wealth than that possessed by all the kings of the world."

"Perhaps." Sam checked to make sure he hadn't missed anything. Then he handed the clock back to Liz. "Let's go get this back where it belongs."

They headed outside. The streets were crowded—it seemed the entire colony had heard of the natives' visit. Dogs were barking in the excitement, and a goat had wandered in and was bleating loudly as a group of boys chased it toward the gate.

"Oh, dear," Liz said as they approached the governor's

house and saw a large group of people gathered in front. "Everyone was over by the church before. It looks as if I may have to sneak in the back way this time."

Just then a shout went up from somewhere in the crowd. "The governor's clock!" a voice cried loudly. "It is gone!"

Sam froze, trading a horrified look with the others. Before he could even blink, more voices called out, and Sam's blood ran cold.

"Thieves!" a howl went up from several voices at once. "The savages are nothing but dirty thieves!"

Twenty-three

"Oh, no!" Liz exclaimed, her face going as white as milk. "They think Powhatan's people stole the clock!"

"Oh, oh, oh!" Hal moaned, looking sick. "Now what are we to do? There shall be war, and we shall all have to move into the fort and live in hovels like Sam's or risk being shot with arrows or clubbed to death in our sleep. . . ."

Sam glanced around, thinking fast. "Pass me the clock," he murmured to Liz.

She did as he said without argument. "Do not do anything foolish, Samuel Gates," she murmured back. "This was my fault, and I'll not have you risk your life."

"I have no intention of risking anyone's life. Except perhaps that dog's." Sam had spotted the blacksmith's black-and-white cur among the dogs in the street. Grabbing him by the scruff of the neck, he dragged the beast off behind a pile of lumber. It whined and wriggled but didn't otherwise protest.

When it emerged a second later, its tail was wagging, and the clock was clenched firmly in its jaws. Another dog spotted its new prize and gave chase, and before long the black-and-white dog was dodging through the crowd chased by its compatriots.

"There you go." Sam walked off toward the back gate, not looking back even when a cry went up as someone spotted the clock. "That's taken care of. Now let's find that treasure."

"I hope we haven't caused too much trouble between our colony and Powhatan's people," Liz said as she, Sam, and Hal picked their way down a steep hill of scree near the river. There had been no time to seek out Matachanna, so they were making their own way across the island as best they could, following the map from the clock casing.

"It should be all right." Sam didn't want her to feel guilty over what she'd done. "Once that dog is blamed— again—things will be no worse than before."

Hal was already panting with exertion, his round face bright red and beaded with sweat. "What does it matter, anyway?" he said. "Better for our people to be suspicious of the savages. Who knows what they might have in mind for us."

Sam ignored him, glancing down at his notebook. "If I'm reading this map right, we should be nearly there," he said. "Ironic, isn't it? All the journeys Gilbert led us on far into the forest, and the treasure was only ten minutes' walk from the fort all along." He smiled and touched the ring hanging about his neck, thinking of his friend Elias, as well as the brother and cousin he'd never met, yet somehow felt he knew. "Too bad Gilbert is gone. I imagine he was quite a fellow."

The map led them to a shady clearing between a sheer rock wall and a grove of tall, narrow pines. Sam had grabbed a pick and spade on their way out of the fort—there was no one in the forge to stop him, as everyone in the settlement was out on the streets—and he quickly dug into the soft ground.

It only took a few minutes to unearth the treasure. "Now, this is more like it!" Hal said between huffs and puffs as he helped Sam haul the large metal-bound trunk out of its hole and into a patch of sunlight. "I've had just about enough of those small boxes! Funny, though—I'd thought a big chest full of gold and jewels might be a bit heavier."

Sam didn't answer. He just stared at the trunk, his heart swelling with pride. He'd done it! He'd worked out the clues, followed the trail Gilbert had laid out so carefully, and ended up here—crouching in front of the treasure. *His* treasure. It was certain that he would remember this feeling for a long, long time to come. Maybe forever. He touched the ring hanging about his neck, wishing that Elias and his brother could know the feeling as well. Maybe in some way, through him, they did.

"Well?" Hal said. "What are you waiting for? Open it and let's see what we've got!"

At that, Sam snapped back to the here and now. Knocking the lock loose with the pick, he lifted the trunk's lid. Hal and Liz leaned forward eagerly.

"Oh," Liz said uncertainly. "Er—what is it?"

For a moment, Sam wasn't sure himself. He dug into the trunk, setting off a cloud of dust. The first item he pulled out was a heavy piece of animal skin decorated with an elaborate pattern of purple and white shell beads and a fringe of feathers. A few of the shells were cracked or loose, and the skin itself showed signs of age, but it was still beautiful.

"Oh," he said. "It looks like some of the things the Powhatans wear. Only older." He blew on it to scatter more of the dust that coated it.

"Who cares?" Hal pushed him aside and reached in himself. "Is there gold beneath it?"

But most of what they pulled out of the trunk was more of the same. There were more beaded objects, beautiful old woven baskets, ropes of necklaces made of shell and bone and horn, and various similar items. At the very bottom lay a handful of old English coins and small mirrors, glass beads, and even some broken metal utensils scuffed with age and hard use.

"None of this junk is worth more than the shoe leather it took to get here!" Hal complained, kicking at the trunk so hard that it sent another puff of dust into the air. "Is this just another clue to the real treasure?"

"I don't think so." Liz was examining what appeared to be a beaded headdress. "These things look quite old. I think this is a native treasure of some sort. It would probably seem of great value to the Powhatan people."

Hal brightened slightly. "Oh, well, that's all right then,

I suppose. At least it's something. Shall we divide it amongst ourselves first, or see about trading it to the savages for food or pelts or something and then divide what we get?"

Sam held up a hand. "I don't feel right about this."

"What do you mean, you don't feel right about it?" Hal looked up from sorting through the handful of coins. "Don't feel right about what?"

Sam hesitated, not sure what he wanted to say. Part of him wanted to keep the treasure he'd worked so hard to find. After all, hadn't he earned it? But another part couldn't help feeling otherwise, especially after what had just happened between the settlers and natives back at the fort.

"It's just—this really would seem a treasure to Powhatan's people, just as Liz said." He spoke slowly as the thoughts formulated in his head. "It's valuable to them—part of their history, like a connection to their ancestors. Finding it would be like us finding, I don't know, that treasure of the ancients Jasper loves to mention. It's more important than just another trunk of Spanish gold. More important than mere money. Do you know what I mean?"

"Sort of." Liz stared at him thoughtfully. "So what do you think we should do with it?"

"Hold on!" Hal protested. "*He's* not deciding anything. We should all get a vote."

Just then they all heard a loud rustling in the trees nearby. "What was that?" Liz asked.

Before the others could answer, Jasper burst into the clearing. And he wasn't alone. He was pushing Matachanna ahead of him, holding her slim arms behind her back with one hand and a knife at her throat with the other.

"Jasper!" Sam cried out. "What are you doing? Let her go!"

Jasper sneered at him. "Well, what do you know," he said. "She tracked you for me, just like a good little savage! Lucky for me I saw her talking with you the other day, isn't it? Now, if you want her to go free, Gates, you and I are going to have to make a deal." Suddenly he noticed the trunk, which Hal had hastily slammed shut at his entrance. "Ah! Then again, perhaps I'll just kill her and then the lot of you as well."

"Wait!" Sam said. "No need for that. We'll hand over the treasure without a fight."

"What?" Hal cried.

"Just let Matachanna go first," Sam said. "Please." He

held his breath, hoping that Jasper would be reasonable. He wouldn't be able to stand it if Matachanna was hurt or killed because of her association with him. Besides, with all the trouble back at the fort, he was sure that was all it would take to blow up any hope of peace.

"Well. . ." Jasper's grip on Matachanna loosened slightly.

Then a voice shouted out suddenly from nearby, making them all jump. Matachanna let out a little cry in response.

"What the—" Jasper muttered, pulling Matachanna closer and setting the knife point at her throat once again.

A moment later Chief Powhatan burst into the clearing, along with several of his warriors. A teenage native girl with long, thick hair and beautiful sad eyes was with them as well; she looked so much like Matachanna that Sam knew right away that this had to be her sister, Matoaka, also known as Pocahontas.

The chief said something in his own language, and Matachanna responded in a trembling voice. Jasper stared at the natives, his hand shaking slightly so that the knife poked at the tender skin of the girl's throat.

"Get away from me, you savages!" he shouted hoarsely. "Don't make me kill her!"

More men burst into the clearing, this time a dozen English settlers led by Governor Gates. Sam spotted his brother among them, along with Sir Dale, Mr. Martin, the tobacco farmer John Rolfe, and other important men of the colony.

"What's going on here?" the governor cried. "Riggs—what are you doing there? Did that girl attack you?"

Chief Powhatan turned to him, his face grim. "He threaten my daughter!" he said in heavily accented English. "He kill her—we kill *all.*" He slashed one hand across his throat to illustrate his meaning.

"I say!" The governor looked insulted. "There's no need for that sort of talk. I thought we'd worked out our differences, at least until that fellow of yours came running in from outside and you lot went racing off without a by-your-leave."

The chief glared at him. Then he turned to Matoaka and said something else in their language.

Matoaka turned to the governor, looking troubled. "My father wishes to be clear. He says you must get that man to release my sister," she said, speaking English as cleanly and clearly as Matachanna did. "Otherwise, there shall be war."

Twenty-four

Sam's heart was racing. The native warriors had closed in behind their chief, their hands already on their weapons. The Englishmen looked nervous; those who carried muskets lifted them slightly. Jasper was wild-eyed as he stared from one group to the other.

"Fine!" he shouted. "Take the nasty savage!"

With that, he shoved Matachanna away from him. She stumbled forward, landing on her hands and knees in the dirt at her sister's feet. A gasp rose from the onlookers.

Matoaka helped Matachanna to her feet. The chief glanced at his daughters, then resumed glaring at the settlers. His men didn't change their stance.

Uh-oh, Sam thought. *Things are still too tense. If someone doesn't do something . . .*

"Wait!" he cried out, realizing that he was the only one who might be able to help. "Look—we found something. Matachanna, tell your father I have a gift for him from— from the people of Jamestown."

Matachanna stared at him in surprise. "What is it, Sam?"

Sam turned and flung open the trunk behind him, ignoring the whimper of protest from Hal. "Chief Powhatan," he said, bowing in what he hoped was a respectful manner. "Please accept this gift. We found it here in the woods."

"What's all this about?" Governor Gates muttered as Matachanna translated Sam's words for her father.

Powhatan stepped forward to peer curiously into the trunk. He murmured something in his language.

"My father says—he says this is a great treasure of our people." This time Matoaka was the one who translated. "He says it was believed lost many seasons ago, long before the time of his father, or his father's father. This treasure—it is our family. Our history. And we thank you for finding it."

The chief picked up the beaded headdress and smiled. He said a few words and his warriors relaxed, loosening their grip on their weapons. It was as if the tension in the clearing had been snuffed like a candle. The only person present who showed no signs of relief was Jasper, who had just been grasped by Thomas Dale and a burly assistant and was now being dragged off toward the fort—and presumably the prison.

"Are you crazy?" Hal said to Sam as the other natives gathered around the trunk, chattering with excitement over the contents. "You had no right to give away our treasure!"

"We had no right to keep it." Sam felt a twinge of sadness. He knew he'd done the right thing. But that didn't make it any less disappointing to allow the treasure to slip out of his hands. "No matter how much we might want to. We had to sacrifice it to save Jamestown."

Liz smiled, then reached out and squeezed his hand. "It was the right thing to do."

Hal swore and stomped away, nearly crashing into William, who was approaching. "What's this about, little brother?" he asked with a smile. "Where did that trunk come from?"

Sam cleared his throat. "Actually, I have been meaning to tell you about that. . . ."

"Excuse me. I'm going to see my father," Liz said, slipping away.

William glanced after her, seeming ready to follow. But

Sam stopped him. "Really," he said. "We need to talk. Or rather, I need to talk, and you may want to listen." With that, he told him the whole story, starting with Elias's letter and ending with digging up the trunk and discovering the natives' treasure. "I wanted to tell you all along," he finished. "I just never found the right time. I'm sorry."

By that time, the natives were preparing to leave. Two of Powhatan's men had hoisted the trunk upon their shoulders to carry it out of the clearing. The chief himself nodded solemnly to Governor Gates before sweeping away with one daughter at either side.

"Odds bodikins!" William swore, looking a bit stunned by Sam's story. "And all this going on with me none the wiser!"

"I'm sorry," Sam said again. "It was wrong of me not to tell you. I just wasn't sure for so long that there really was a treasure at all, and then once Jasper tried to blame you for that theft, I felt terrible for having involved you so unwittingly, especially after all that happened back home with Father. . . ."

William nodded, his face solemn. "I understand. It's one thing to sail for another world to escape one's family shame.

Quite another to flee it within one's own mind." He broke into a smile and slapped his brother on the back. "But don't worry over me; no harm done. Besides, you did it, Sammy! You solved all those dastardly clues and found the treasure!"

"Yes, and it was all for nothing," he mumbled, watching the natives disappear among the trees. "So much for the vast riches Elias was hoping to find."

"Never mind." William glanced around, looking distracted. "Say, where did Liz get to?"

Sam gulped. "Er, that's one other thing I want to talk to you about." Before he could lose his nerve, he went on. "I—I have been enjoying Liz's company for some time. That is, I find her most, well, I mean ever since I first made her acquaintance, I think of her often. And so then you mentioned wishing to court her, and I did not speak then but . . ." He trailed off, feeling uncharacteristically tongue-tied.

"I see." William gazed at him, rubbing his chin. "So you're sweet on the young lady, eh?"

Sam held his breath. It was almost always easy to tell what William was thinking, but at the moment his face was a cipher. Was he angry? Or was he perhaps scoffing at him for his soft feelings, thinking that such foolishness had no place in this rough, practical world?

"All right, then," William said abruptly. "I shall not stand in your way. I want only what's best for my only brother."

"Truly?" Sam didn't quite dare to believe it. "You do not mind? I do not wish this to stand between us, William. I know you had hopes. . . ."

William chuckled. "Indeed," he said, pulling out a sheet of paper. "However, my hopes have lately changed. Mother and Father wrote us—the letter arrived by supply ship this morning. They tell me Mary Wallis is coming to Jamestown by the next ship with the family that employs her. They will all be settling here."

"Oh!" Suddenly Sam understood. Mary was a young lady of William's acquaintance from back in London. She had grown up on their street before going to live as a ladies' maid at a wealthy gentleman's home nearby.

William shrugged, looking a bit sheepish. "Mary shall not make the same sort of financial match as Miss Martin would," he said. "But I have always found her most agreeable and flatter myself that she feels the same." He laughed.

"Perhaps she will," Sam said with a smile.

"Here." William handed over the letter. "I've already

read it. All is well at home; Father is slowly paying off his debt and still hopes to join us here one day."

Sam skimmed the letter, happy to see his father's familiar spiky writing interspersed with his mother's loopier script. It reminded him of the way his parents had taught him reading and writing by turns, his mother finding such a thing natural due to her higher birthright, his father wishing his sons to lack no advantages in life beyond those they could not help. . . .

I suppose it's true, that phrase I read in Mr. Davison's book of poems, Sam thought with a pang. *Absence makes the heart grow fonder.*

With that, his nostalgic thoughts wandered to the little bookbinder's shop where he'd sat upon a stool many nights after hours, poring over all sorts of texts and dreaming of adventure and faraway lands. That young man had had no idea what was in store for him—or what type of riches the New World held.

His gaze wandered to Liz. She was still talking with her father nearby. *I am not that boy upon the stool anymore,* Sam realized.

Just then the governor approached him. "Young Mr. Gates," he said. "This colony owes you a debt of gratitude. I do not know where you acquired those native things, but be sure that I shall not forget this."

"I appreciate that, sir," Sam said, part of his mind still back in London. "But if you please, part of any credit owed belongs to the entire Gates family. After all, I am who I am because of them."

An hour later, Sam was standing at the river's edge near the Martin plantation.

"I still can't believe you gave away our treasure," Hal complained. "All that effort, and we're left with nothing!"

"What effort are you on about?" Liz frowned at him. "All the effort was Sam's and mine—all you did was follow us about and complain."

"That's not true," Hal argued. "I was the one who got the clock clue, wasn't I? If not for me you two might still be standing there trying to work it out."

Sam wasn't listening. He'd just spotted Matachanna emerging from the trees on the opposite shore. "Please come with me!" she called to them. "My father wishes to see you."

Hal's eyes grew wide. "Not me," he cried. "I've had enough of savages for one day. I'll not set foot near their village!" With that, he turned and ran toward the house.

Liz rolled her eyes heavenward. "Shall we go chase him down and drag him along by the ear?"

"Don't bother," Sam said with a smile, though he felt a twinge of nervousness at the memory of Chief Powhatan's imposing presence. "We can go without him."

Soon they were walking through the forest with Matachanna. "I am not sure what my father wishes of you," she told them. "But I can assure you, he is not angry."

Sure enough, when Sam and Liz entered the village they were immediately greeted by a smiling Chief Powhatan. The trunk was sitting near the community fire pit with its contents spread out around it. Dozens of natives were gathered around examining the items, from tiny children to a woman so old and wrinkled that she appeared to be carved out of wood.

"Welcome, my friends," Chief Powhatan said in English. Then he turned and gestured behind him, and Matoaka appeared. He said a few words to her and then she smiled at the visitors.

"My father, the great Wahunsunacock, wishes to give you both greatest thanks for returning the riches of our ancestors," she said. The chief spoke again, and she continued to translate. "Some of the eldest members of our village remember tales of these treasures, though all thought they were lost forever."

The ancient woman spoke up, her voice as soft and rapid as a breeze. Matoaka and Powhatan both turned toward her respectfully, listening. When the woman had finished, she turned to smile at the English visitors with a mouth completely empty of teeth.

"Our wise grandmother says that your actions have righted an ancient wrong," Matoaka said to Sam and Liz. "It was said that the first people of your kind found this treasure buried far from here. But rather than returning it to our people, they hid it again." She glanced at the old woman uncertainly. "And that is why they were cursed by the gods and seen no more on these shores. . . . Grandmother, I don't understand."

"I think I do," Sam said thoughtfully, glancing at Liz. "It sounds as if she's saying the treasure was hidden long ago, but uncovered by the settlers at Roanoke—the Lost Colony—back in 1587 or thereabouts. I suppose that's the meaning of that part of Gilbert's letter, as well—Elias did mention something of a note from their Uncle James. James must have been among those who hid it. It's a mystery how it got up here for Gilbert to find, so far from Roanoke, but I suppose many things about the Lost Colony are a mystery. . . ."

His voice trailed off. Chief Powhatan was staring at him in bewilderment, and even Matoaka and Matachanna, who at least could understand most of his words, looked a bit confused. Sam smiled.

"Er, never mind," he said. "Matoaka, Matachanna, please tell your father that I am honored by his thanks."

"Ah, but that is not all." Matoaka said a few words in her own language, and several warriors came forward carrying something wrapped in an entire deer's hide. "My father wishes he could present you with something as valuable as what you have given us. But he hopes you will be satisfied with this token."

Powhatan said a few words in his language, then bowed before Sam and Liz. "I hope you take this as my thanks," he said in his broken English. "It is all I have to offer."

He made a sharp hand gesture toward the warriors. They stepped in front of Sam and Liz and dumped the contents of the deerskin on the ground before them. Old English coins, dented metal spoons, and other items bounced out onto the ground.

"It is merely the English bits from the trunk you found," Matoaka said. "These things mean little to us, but my father thought it right that your ancestors' things be returned to you as ours were to us."

"Thank you." Sam smiled at Matoaka, then at the chief. "Please tell your father he is most generous." From his previous glimpse of the items, he knew they didn't add up to enough to be considered a true treasure. But he was still happy to have them, if only as a memento of his first weeks in the New World.

"Wait, what's this?" Liz kneeled down to grab something from the pile. "I don't remember seeing it before."

Matachanna peered at it. "That was stuck onto the beading of one of the ceremonial cloaks," she said. "It fell out when Grandmother tried it on."

Sam gasped when he saw what Liz was holding. It was a large gold ring encrusted with jewels of every description.

"Zounds!" Liz exclaimed. "I've never seen anything like it!"

Sam peered at the ring. "It must be Spanish," he said. "I wonder how it got in with the other things?"

"What does it matter?" Liz grinned. "This is what I call a treasure! It must be worth an unimaginable amount!"

Sam realized she was right. Even a small part of that ring would surely be more than enough to pay off his father's debt and bring him and Mother to the New World.

"Zounds, indeed!" he cried, impulsively grabbing Liz and kissing her.

Then, realizing what he'd done, he pulled away. They were not even officially courting!

But Liz merely laughed—and pulled him closer to kiss again.

Powhatan was beaming at them, seeming pleased by their excitement. For a moment Sam wondered if it was right to accept the ring from the natives, considering how much it had to be worth.

Then he realized that didn't matter. To Powhatan's people, such things as gold and jewels held little worth at all. To them, such things truly were a token in comparison to the treasure Sam had found.

So this makes everyone satisfied with their lot, Sam thought, watching as Liz tried the ring on her finger and held it up to admire in the sunlight. *It is the same way the raccoon does not value the same things as the bird. That is why there is room for both of them in the forest, just as there is room for both our peoples in this great, rich, wonderful land.*

Liz smiled at him, waggling the ring on her hand. "Shall we tell Hal of this? Or keep it a secret between us?"

Sam laughed, knowing she was joking. "I suppose we must tell him," he joked in return. "But perhaps we don't have to tell him how much it's *really* worth."

As they were gathering up their treasure into its deerskin, the elderly woman came up to them, leaning heavily on a gnarled tree branch she used as a cane. She crooked one bony finger, summoning Matachanna over.

"Our grandmother wonders if you would be so kind as to help her," Matachanna said. "She wishes to learn your language—my sister has been helping her practice."

"Of course!" Sam was a little surprised that someone so old should care to undertake such a project as learning a new language. Then again, he understood very well the thirst for knowledge, for new experiences. After all, that was what had led him to this spot.

"Good afternoon," the old woman said in her soft, wavery voice, pronouncing each word carefully. "We thank you for what you have done."

"You are welcome." Sam bowed respectfully. "Your English is very good."

The old woman nodded to acknowledge the compliment. Then she glanced around to see if anyone was listening before leaning closer. "Your gold," she said, indicating the ring on Liz's hand. "It is only a token."

"Yes, I understand," Sam said. "But we do appreciate it."

"No, no!" The old woman shook her head, appearing frustrated. Turning to Matachanna, she rattled off several sentences in her own tongue.

Matachanna shrugged. "Grandmother says there is more treasure like that," she reported. "But it is no longer here. She says when she was younger, she saw your people traveling past this place." She wrinkled her brow, looking confused, then asked a question in her own tongue.

"I saw them!" the old woman insisted, shaking her bony fist. "With mine own eyes I saw the pale faces going by. I knew not then where from, or where to. But they did go." She gestured toward the northwest.

Sam and Liz exchanged a glance. "Is she talking about the Roanoke colonists?" Liz wondered.

Matachanna shook her head. "Grandmother's mind is sharp, but she has spent many years telling stories to entertain the children," she said. "I'm not sure she remembers what is tale and what is truth anymore."

"I spoke to one!" the old woman burst out, her eyes far away as if looking into the past. "He tell me of riches—great riches, as large as all the wealth of all the tribes. He was leaving to seek it over all the land."

"Yes, Grandmother," Matachanna said, switching into her own language as she steered the woman over to a log to sit down.

Liz smiled at Sam. "I suppose we should go if we wish to get home before sundown."

"Yes," Sam agreed, still watching the old woman. "Let us go home."

They tied up their bundle of treasure, and Sam slung it over his shoulder. Then they thanked the chief once more, said good-bye to Matoaka and the others, and prepared to head back to Jamestown with Matachanna as their guide.

The elderly woman was still sitting on her log, and Sam

walked over to her on his way past. "Farewell, Grandmother," he said, bowing. "It was nice talking with you. I hope we shall get another chance to converse."

She reached into her skirt. "One more treasure for you, young friend," she said, pressing something into his hand. "He gave it to me that night—long ago. He said it marked the treasure he gave up to seek the larger."

"Thank you." Sam smiled at her, then backed away.

Once he'd rejoined Liz and Matachanna, he looked to see what the old woman had given him. "What's that?" Liz asked.

"I'm not sure." He studied the item, which was a little smaller than a clock face. "It seems to be some kind of wooden medallion. But look—is that a drawing on it?"

Liz laughed. "Oh, dear," she said. "Do not tell me it is a clue to another treasure!"

Sam smiled and tucked the little wooden item away for further study later. He wasn't sure what it was, or if it meant anything at all that his heart pounded a bit faster when he glanced at it. But if it did have something to do with a treasure, he surely do all he could to find it. In the meantime, he was looking forward to telling William that their family would soon be together once again.

"Come," he said, grasping Liz's hand and squeezing it, feeling the hard shape of the Spanish ring against his palm. "Let's get home to Jamestown."

Post Script

Like the films *National Treasure* and *National Treasure: Book of Secrets* that inspired it, this is a fictional story grounded in real facts and history. Samuel Gates, Elizabeth and Hal Martin, and some of the other characters, are invented, but many others who appear in the story were real people who lived at that time.

For instance, most people have heard of Captain John Smith and his friend Pocahontas, also known as Matoaka. Pocahontas's father, Wahunsunacock, known as Chief Powhatan, was also a real person, as was his brother Opechancanough, who became head of the Powhatan Confederacy when Wahunsunacock died in 1618. Matachanna was also real; little is known about her, but she is recorded as Pocahontas's sister or half-sister. Wingina, mentioned here in connection with the Roanoke colony, was also a real figure (though his headdress as described in *Changing Tides* is fictional). Throughout, Powhatan is used to describe both the tribe and the chief.

Governor Thomas Gates and his marshall, Sir Thomas Dale, really were the leaders of Jamestown in 1612. The set of strict laws known as Dale's Code was in force from 1611 to 1619. Dale took over as governor of Jamestown when Gates returned to England in 1614.

John Rolfe was also real; his export of a new strain of tobacco in 1612 was a breakthrough for the colony. He arrived in Jamestown with Thomas Gates in 1610, just after the Starving Time, and later established a plantation upriver from the fort. In 1614, Rolfe married Pocahontas, who then changed her name to Rebecca Rolfe; this brought about a period of peace between the Powhatan and the settlers.

And of course, everyone has heard of William Shakespeare! His play, *The Tempest*, was first performed in 1611. Many people believe it was based on the shipwreck of Captain Christopher Newport's *Sea Venture* in Bermuda (with Thomas Gates and John Rolfe aboard), which delayed the arrival of vital supplies in Jamestown by nearly a year and almost led to the failure of the colony.

Many other real-life figures of that time period are mentioned here in passing, even though they don't actually appear in the story. These include Sir Walter Raleigh, Christopher Newport, Baron De La Warr (for whom the state of Delaware is named), John Ratcliffe, King James I, John White, Christopher Marlowe, John Donne, Cervantes, Reverend Whitaker, and Ralph Lane.

Archaeological evidence of the original Jamestown fort is still being discovered at its site; it really was triangular in shape, and some of the other details here have been gleaned from various sources.

The *Susan Constant* was a real ship; along with the *Godspeed* and the *Discovery*, she landed at what was to become Jamestown in 1607. The *Susan Constant* is known to have made several journeys between England and Virginia, though the details of the journey depicted in this book (including Captain Bradford and John White's lantern) are fictional.

The Lost Colony of Roanoke is a well-known historical mystery; to this day, nobody knows what became of Virginia Dare and the rest of the settlers who disappeared sometime between John White's departure in 1587 and his return in 1590. The only clue was the word CROATOAN carved at the abandoned settlement and the letters CRO carved elsewhere nearby.

Finally, there really was an outbreak of the black death (aka bubonic plague) in London in 1608 which closed the theaters.

Many of the other people and events have been invented for this story, though we have tried to remain true in most ways to the historical realities of how people lived at the time.

DON'T MISS THE NEXT VOLUME...

MIDNIGHT RIDE

❧ *A* GATES *Family Mystery* ❧

John Raleigh Gates wants nothing to do with treasure. For too long he has been embarrassed by his father's obsession with hidden wealth and coded messages. With the American colonies on the verge of war with Britian, John is more concerned with the future than the past.

So when John's job as a post rider puts him in contact with a group of Patriots—including a quiet man named Paul Revere—he sees it as his chance to step out from under his father's shadow. But a dying man's last words quickly thrust John into a hunt greater than any his father could imagine. Now, as the colonies prepare to fight for their freedom, John must set out on the ride of his life and find a treasure that could make a nation.